THE Devil YOU KNOW

HELLFIRE
BOOK ONE

JENA GREGOIRE

THE DEVIL YOU KNOW
Hellfire Book One
© 2018 Jena Gregoire

ISBN 13: 978-1481182089

Published by Jena Gregoire
Cover by Dark Mojo Designs
Print Formatting by The Madd Formatter
Editing by Modern Elektra Editing

JenaGregoire.com

CHAPTER ONE

Michael

Michael laid on his back, staring at the ceiling of Deziree's darkened bedroom. The hot night air was thick and damp. The spinning slowed as the effects of the alcohol began to wear off. *Finally*, he thought. His patience was wearing thin. No matter how much water he consumed, the drunken state he had been in all night just didn't want to let go. Normally this wasn't a concern that would even register on his radar, but tonight was different. Tonight they had done something and crossed a line. Tonight he had slept with Deziree. His oldest friend. An action which irrevocably changed things between them. Forever. He just wasn't sure if it was a change for the better or worse.

Four centuries is a long time to know someone. It's also four hundred years of friendship that gets flushed down the drain if they're not on the same page. No sooner had that thought crossed his mind, he began to question himself.

Did you want this to happen?

Well, yes. He'd be lying if he said he'd never considered it before. Hell, they'd even come dangerously close to something happening a few times in the first hundred years they knew each other. Why not? She's Dez. She's beautiful with her long black hair, flawless skin, ice-blue eyes, and that body....

She was hard and lethal. Her form was toned and well-conditioned. Despite her average size, she could hold her own against just about anyone. However, the muscle didn't make her look masculine by any stretch of the imagination. She had generous curves in all the right places. In his eyes, she was the embodiment of the word sexy. Last night, he had found out just how perfect that word was.

He had been hired to get rid of a problem for one of his clients. The problem was an amateur extortionist who thought he could get away with trying to blackmail one of the wealthiest criminals in New York. When you have as much money and power as this particular client, blackmail doesn't work. It's usually just a fast pass to an early grave. Luckily for the man, Michael hadn't received his usual call from this particular client. He didn't want the guy taken out, just scared off. He'd been trailing the guy on and off for about a week to get a sense of his habits. He was getting ready to go confront his mark when his cell phone rang.

"Hey, Vegas," she greeted as soon as the line picked up. She almost never waited for him to say hello anymore. Even without the aid of the caller ID, he would have known who was on the line simply by her voice. "I'm bored out of fucking my mind. What are you up to tonight?"

"I thought you had a job coming up," he replied. She'd been mentioning it for weeks. "Shouldn't you be out committing a Class A felony right about now?"

"I'm still waiting on a confirmation from the buyer. For a guy with too much money to ever have to worry about money, he sure likes to drag his feet when buying gifts for his wife. Or his mistress. I'm not sure which it is this time. Anyway, do you want to go do something? I can't sit

2

around here anymore, and I think I make Jack nervous when I hang around Onyx."

He was about to tell her he couldn't make it when he was hit with a stroke of genius. "Dez," he said with a smile, "put on something slutty. We're going out." After a quick shower, he put on a pair of his most comfortable dark blue jeans, a black button-down shirt, and his favorite pair of butter-colored Timberland boots. After slipping on his glittering platinum and diamond-encrusted watch, he grabbed his black leather jacket and headed for the door.

He knew there was no hiding his reaction when he had arrived at her place. She opened the door, and he found himself utterly speechless. She stood there in a black sequined halter top, form-fitting black patent leather pants, and a pair of sexy black stiletto heels. She topped the whole outfit with a leather bolero jacket that looked like something out of a Mad Max movie. Deziree was dressed to kill and she was stunning. He stood there staring like a fool, momentarily at a loss for words.

"Wow, Dez. You look sensational."

Dez smiled and with a wink, she replied, "You don't look so bad yourself." Then she added with more seriousness, "Now, pick your jaw up off the floor and wipe the drool off your chin. We are going out, right?"

"Not exactly. I'll explain in the car." She glared at him with suspicion. "You'll love it," he promised. "Shall we?"

He held his hand out for her to walk ahead of him. He took in the sight of her and his priorities shifted. Suddenly, going to work was the last thing on his mind. They made their way down to his Aston Martin waiting for them by the curb. As they approached the car, he reached around her, purposely leaning in close while he reached for the handle. He held the door as she carefully slid into the passenger seat. He closed the door and hurried to the other side to climb into the driver's seat. The crimson red

Vantage boasted a V12 with far more power than any car its size needed. The engine roared to life with the pressure of the crystal key in the center console. He had a few cars stored in various high-priced private garages around the city, but this was one of his favorites. You couldn't help but feel good when you were behind the wheel.

They had only driven a few minutes when Dez started demanding answers. "So? What does 'not exactly' mean?" He explained the job to her and how he wanted to approach it. When the plan was all laid out for her, Deziree smiled like the Cheshire Cat. She clasped her hands together and bounced in her seat. "Oh, this is going to be way more fun than just going out and getting drunk." He couldn't help but laugh. He had expected the plan would go over well, but was not prepared for bouncing.

The nightclub was packed. The main parking lot was full, and there was a line out the door and halfway around the block. The place was trendy enough that they had valet service. They climbed out of the car and Michael slipped the valet a crisp hundred dollar bill. As he did so, he pulled the man closer and whispered in his ear, "One scratch and I'll snap your neck." Michael backed off and smiled. "Savvy?" The young man nervously nodded his head. "Good. Now, keep my keys handy. I don't know how long we are going to be here." Michael walked around to Deziree and presented the crook of his arm.

She smiled, looped her arm through, and said, "Game on." They ascended the steps of the massive brick building.

The facade of the building gave a completely false impression of what lay concealed within its walls. Judging by the black-painted brick walls and scarce lighting, a stranger to the club would probably expect a dirty, unkempt grunge-rock club. They couldn't be further off the mark. The interior was lavishly decorated to emulate

4

an old bordello. The plush leather and velvet seats were accented by warm red and purple lighting. The whole place gave off a vibe of pure sensuality.

Had they been prepared for the sheer number of bodies in the room, Michael probably wouldn't have chosen the club as the location to approach the guy. He knew they'd be busy, but they had to be way over capacity. He suggested they grab a table, and they were able to get a perfect spot at the back, up on a slightly elevated level, only a few steps above the main floor. It was a perfect vantage point to scan the room for their target. He slid into the plush leather crescent-shaped booth and waved a waitress over. He ordered their usual drinks and surveyed the crowd. A sweep to the left. A sweep to the right. Then his eyes landed on Dez.

He hadn't realized when she'd slipped away. A quick glance at the other half of the booth told him she had shed her jacket and immediately took to the hunt. She moved through the crowd with a grace the humans could only wish to match. Without even trying, she commanded the attention of the patrons, male and female alike. She searched out her prey with the skill of a master predator. Had he not known what she was, he would have pegged her for a vampire from a distance.

Michael smiled to himself as he watched her dance her way through the crowd. Once upon a time, he'd seen her as so much more than a friend. Every time they'd come close to anything resembling romance or sexual tension, something was always off. The timing wasn't right or whatever the excuse of the day happened to be. Sometimes it was her hang up, sometimes it was his. When they just couldn't seem to get it right, they gave up on the idea of being together, no matter how easy it should have been. The thought brought him up short with a sense of longing — and mourning. Mourning for a life they could have shared. They had made the decision together to keep things friendly, but every once in a while, regret clawed at him. He thought he was making the right decision at the time, but more than once, he second guessed himself.

He continued to watch Dez. She stopped at one point to buy a shot off of a waitress attempting to snake her way past a crowd of, assumedly, drunk frat boys. The petite blonde seemed grateful for the reprieve from dodging flailing elbows.

Dez locked eyes with him and nodded her head towards the bar. Michael followed her line of sight and saw what had her attention. It was difficult to see the man's face from the way he was sitting at the bar. He took one brief look over his shoulder at the dance floor, and Michael had the confirmation he needed that she had found the right guy. In the car, he had given her as accurate a description as he possibly could without actually showing her pictures, and she had picked him out of the crowd faster than Michael would have guessed possible. He nodded to her discreetly, and she smiled with an arched eyebrow and then turned her attention back to her mission.

Michael chuckled and took a sip of his drink. *Poor fucker is never going to know what hit him.*

He watched as Dez worked her magic. She had her target and nothing was going to stop her now. She worked her way slowly through the crowd toward the guy without making it obvious she was after him. That sexy little strut of hers grabbed the attention of their mark in no time, and she took the opportunity to make eye contact. Dez smiled at him coyly and eased toward him. Once she reached him, she came up behind his seat, bent in close, and whispered in his ear. Michael felt pangs of something he never expected. Jealousy.

As Dez pulled back from him, the guy looked awestruck. He nodded enthusiastically to whatever she said. Deziree was probably the last woman on Earth he would have expected to come on to him. Little did he know, he was in for a big surprise. Michael watched as she took the man by the hand and led him down a hallway tucked away in a shadowy corner of the busy room.

While Deziree was gone, Michael couldn't help but let his mind wander to what could have been. Triggered simply by her proximity to another man, a man Michael knew full well was about to wish he had never laid eyes on her. It had been years since he'd had those types of feelings for her and yet, there they were.

Before he could marinate in hypotheticals, Dez emerged from the hallway, alone and smiling. She weaved her way through the dance floor of gyrating bodies to their table. She picked up her drink and took nearly the entire glass in one gulp.

"So?" Michael looked at her expectantly.

"Not going to be a problem anymore," Deziree assured him as she set her glass on the table and waved a waitress over. "As it turns out, Mr. Roberts would very much appreciate the ability to maintain his position on the mortal plane." She took four shots from the waitress's tray. They were the novelty kind in plastic test tubes, each one filled with a different brightly-colored mixture. She dropped a fifty dollar bill on the tray and the woman started to dig out change. "You're all set," Dez purred and winked at the buxom brunette.

Deziree enthusiastically downed the first shot, and then leaned forward and smiled at Michael. "Did you know," she started as she held her hand up in front of him, "there are twenty-seven bones in a human hand?"

Michael looked at her hand in confusion.

"Not that I'm against higher learning, but why am I getting an anatomy lesson in a bar?"

"Well," Deziree explained, "not to brag or anything,

but I just broke fifty-four bones in that gentleman's body. Oddly enough, by the time I was through with the second hand, Mr. Roberts no longer had any interest in pursuing his recent activities involving your client." She drank down her second shot and smiled, obviously proud of herself. "Sadly, I do believe Mr. Happy is going to be quite neglected for some time. Serves the man right, all things considered. Thinking with that particular head is what landed him in that nasty little room with me in the first place. When I left, he was headed for the back exit. I imagine he's going to need some help with that door handle."

Michael shook his head and smiled. He should have known she would have something like that planned. He took his two shots and glanced around for the waitress. "This calls for a celebration."

The rest of the evening had been spent drinking and dancing. The more alcohol they tossed back, the further their carefully-held restraints blurred. By the time they left the club, their usual harmless flirting had turned into shameless making out and hands that just would not keep to themselves. Rather than chance getting kicked out for public indecency, they decided it was time to leave. Vegas retrieved the keys to his car from the valet attendant, and then hailed one of the many idling taxis waiting outside for intoxicated patrons.

One tense and silence-riddled car ride later, they were back at Deziree's apartment. The trip did little to cool them off. Michael could feel his extended fangs pushing against the inside of his bottom lip. He kept his mouth closed in an attempt to hide his steadily-growing arousal, but there wasn't much he could do to hide his eyes. His normally rich golden irises cast a bright glow which was impossible to miss. He glanced at Dez and caught the smirk playing at the edge of her lips.

Deziree led the way into the building, up the stairs, and to the door. As she fumbled with the lock, Michael stepped back and leaned against the wall. He tipped his head, allowing his eyes to roam over every inch of her lithe body, taking in every arc and curve. He had spent the entire evening with those curves pressed up against him and now he wanted more. He imagined running his hands and mouth over her soft, naked skin and felt the sharp points of his teeth extend further.

When she finally won the battle against her keys, Dez turned around, grabbed him by the shirt, and tugged him into the apartment. As soon as the metal door closed behind them, Michael lost any semblance of control. A low growl escaped from deep in his chest as he spun, pinning her up against the cool steel, and he kissed her hard, one of his fangs scraping her bottom lip, just barely breaking the skin. The aroma of her blood drove him further out of his mind.

As their mouths met, passion exploded between the two of them; a passion of which, until now, he hadn't been aware. There had always been a latent attraction between them, but this was animal. Primal. Feral. Passion quickly gave way to urgency as they stripped each other's clothes off. After unsuccessfully trying to remove his shirt in the conventional way, she gave up and yanked it open, ripping three buttons off in the process, sending them scattering across the floor.

"Dez," Michael began, pulling back slightly. In the midst of his drunken haze, a thought crossed his mind. *What if we're making a mistake?*

"Shut up," she quickly replied in a breathy voice.

She grabbed a fistful of each side of his open shirt and guided him back to her. She ran her hands up his bare tattooed chest and he closed his eyes, allowing himself to feel every sensation. She lightly ran her fingertips up his neck, along his jaw, and finally caressed his lips. He couldn't take anymore. He grasped the sides of her face and crushed his mouth to hers. They finally gave in to a need they had both been trying to ignore for far too long. They weren't even able to make it to the bedroom the first time.

Michael glanced over at Deziree's sleeping form as all the memories of the previous hours continued to dance through his mind. He had wanted this, wanted her, so intensely for years, and he'd worked very hard to bury those feelings and pretend they didn't exist. Now he had to wonder if this meant he was actually within reach of the life he dreamt of so long ago. *Is it safe to even think that way?* He had no idea how Dez was going to feel about this when she finally woke up. *She may write it off as a one-night slip caused by far too much alcohol.* He knew he didn't feel the same way, and he dreaded the conversation that would undoubtedly follow. He didn't want the spark of hope simmering in his core to be extinguished.

Michael's thoughts were interrupted by his cell phone ringing in the other room. In the silent house, "Dirty Deeds" cut through the air and the AC/DC song serving as his ringtone seemed much louder than it really was. He eased off the bed, careful not to wake Dez with his movement. While in the throes of passion, he hadn't been particularly focused on where his phone had been thrown. The ringing song came to an end just as he clicked on a small table lamp. It was quiet for about ten seconds when the ringing started again. *Must be important.* He followed the incessant noise and eventually found the phone under the edge of the couch.

"This is Michael," he answered, voice still gravelly from sleep and too much Captain Morgan. He listened as the caller hurriedly explained why he was needed. "I will be on the first flight out." The caller thanked him and disconnected.

Michael gathered his things and put on his clothes. He went back into the bedroom, contemplating whether or not to wake up Deziree and let her know he was leaving. Fear of the impending conversation made the decision for him and he resolved to call her later in the day, after he landed. He quietly made his exit from the bedroom, making his way to the front door and stepped out into the night to retrieve his Aston Martin from across town.

CHAPTER TWO

Dez

Deziree opened her eyes and pain rocketed through her skull. She winced and closed her lids tight, rubbing her temples. She opened them again, only just enough to steal a glance at her bedside alarm clock. It was six in the morning: far too early to be awake after the night she'd had. She shut her eyes again and rolled over, expecting to feel the warmth of another body beside her. Instead, she was greeted with cold sheets and no Vegas. *Maybe he's making coffee. I could seriously use some coffee.* She blinked away the sleep and leaned up on her elbows, listening for the shuffling noises of life in her apartment. Nothing but the steady pounding in her head.

"Vegas?" she called out, much to her own detriment.

When she received no response, Dez climbed out of her bed and threw on her worn-out Nine Inch Nails t-shirt. The front of the shirt was emblazoned with their signature logo in blue, and on the back, it simply said *like an animal…* The shirt was ratty and stained but it was so comfortable, she refused to give it up. Coupled with a pair of panties, she was dressed enough to wander the house without giving any neighbors a free peep show.

She passed her vacant bathroom, walked out into the living room, and found that Vegas was not making coffee. In fact, Vegas was nowhere to be found. She grabbed the phone off her kitchen counter and dialed a number so ingrained in her, she didn't even need to think about what buttons to push. She put the phone to her ear and listened. Instead of ringing, she was greeted by his voicemail message.

"You have reached the voicemail of Michael Tremayne. Please leave your name and number, and I will get back to you as soon as I can."

Beeeeeeeep

Dez hung up without leaving a message. She didn't know what to think.

"Son of a ..."

Had he actually left in the middle of the night without a word? This was not the Vegas she knew. Even if he did regret what happened the night before, he wouldn't have just left without saying anything. There must have been a reason.

Deziree took the phone with her back into the bedroom. If he tried to call while she was sleeping off her hangover, she wanted to be able to take the call without traveling too far from the comfort of her pillow. She climbed back into bed and as she shut her eyes, Vegas was on her mind.

There must be a reason.

CHAPTER THREE

Dez

5 ... 4... 3... 2... 1... ... ...

"Charlie, you dumb shit!" She rounded on her accomplice to find him looking angry. She'd half expected him to be cowering and apologetic. Instead, he was angrily pawing through his box of goodies looking for what she could only assume was going to be a fix for their little problem.

"Explosives, Charlie. Aren't they supposed to, you know, explode?" She tried to make an exaggerated expanding circle motion with her arms. "Not fucking impressed."

"I'm looking, I'm looking," he mumbled. With a sour scowl on his face, he continued to rifle through the tool box. Deziree eyed him with suspicion. This foul mood and surly demeanor were not the type of behavior she'd grown to expect from Charlie. He was always so calm and laid-back when they were on jobs.

"Charlie, do you know why I like you so much?" The glare he aimed at her told Deziree he was annoyed and certainly didn't want to cooperate with her line of questioning. "You're the best explosives guy in the business, you value money more than your own life and, as such, your fealty goes to the highest bidder. As it happens, that's usually me. More important than all that is you're frightened of me. Since I pay a king's ransom every time I hire you, and I could still easily kick your ass, what could you possibly have your panties in a bunch over right now that's got you so out of sorts?"

"My panties are just fine, thank you very much, and I won't have you insulting my work. Say what you want about me personally, but my work is solid. Now, if you'll excuse me for a moment, I need to find out where the problem lies."

She watched him return to his task and allowed her mind to drift. She wondered where Vegas had gotten off to for the past week and then quickly pushed him out of her head, mentally scolding herself for allowing him to take up even a fraction of her thoughts. *You need to accept the fact that you were a one-night stand, and he did what every normal guy does.* Only he was not a normal guy and she knew it.

"Ahhhh, here we are!" Charlie traced through the wiring and suddenly turned, breaking her away from her thoughts. He was holding what appeared to be a broken gadget of some sort. "Dez, tell me something? How is it that you are a top-shelf thief and a cold-blooded killer when the circumstances call for it, but you don't notice when you step on and crush an expensive piece of high-end circuitry? Hmm?"

Immediately on the defensive, she placed her hands on her hips and demanded "How do you know it was me?"

"Let's see. I would bet my *king's ransom*, as you so eloquently put it, the hole in the top of the casing precisely fits the heel of your impractical stiletto boots." The look he was giving her was an outright challenge to protest. With fleeting satisfaction and a switch to intensely serious, he nearly growled. "That's what I thought. Never question the quality of my work again, bunched panties or not."

"Fine," she replied. "Let's just get this done and get out of here. We will liberate the bracelet from its jailor—"

"You mean steal it from its owner," he corrected with a smirk.

"Semantics, Charles. Once this job is done, we will both get a fat payday and then you can take some time off." That got his attention.

"Really?" The word was loaded with far more surprise and enthusiasm than she was anticipating.

"Yes," she replied, eying him curiously. "Why?"

"You don't take time off."

"Well," she replied, "I'm ready for a vacation."

She watched as he thought about that for a moment, then he relaxed and set down what he was working on.

"I'm out, Dez."

"What do you mean, 'you're out'?" she cautiously inquired.

"For a little while, at least. I believe it's time. I have ties here now which I am not willing to walk away from, and she's a mortal. Since their lives are so abbreviated, I want to spend what time I can with her." The look on his face was resolved yet sad. "I am also finding I am not fully enjoying this work anymore. It's become *just* work. The money is good, but I don't really need it. I haven't needed it for quite some time, actually. I'm sure I will come back one day. Until then, you can consider me on an indefinite hiatus."

Deziree was unexpectedly sad at the news. She and Charlie had always worked well together, but she hadn't thought of him as much more than a work associate. The deep disappointment setting up shop on the pit of her stomach took her by surprise. She swallowed down the lump in her throat and tried to ignore her eyes, which were threatening to well up with tears.

She cleared her throat, and awkwardly responded, "Well, don't get any ideas in your head about going-away parties or a farewell *shag*. That's not my style." Then with an affectionate smile, she added, "I'm going to miss you."

Charlie wasn't letting her off the hook that easily.

"Deziree Davanzati! Was that you expressing, dare I say, an *emotion*? Keep it up and I won't be scared of you anymore. Could this possibly have something to do with that bloodsucker you've been spending so much time with? What's his name? Reno?"

"Charlie, you know full well his name is Vegas. Well, Michael, actually. And no, he's not the reason. And that most certainly was not emotion. That was me expressing appreciation for an asset in the business." *You just keep telling yourself that*, she thought.

Charlie smirked, obviously not buying her story. "Yes, well, at any rate, I'm going to miss you too." He paused and then added, "Dearly, in fact."

CHAPTER FOUR

Dez

After raining for the previous two days, the constant barrage of water had finally come to an end. *Just in time to have to go to work*, she thought while glancing in her car's rear view mirror. The downside to living in New York City was the completely unpredictable northeast weather during the summer. The forecast could call for sunny, cloudless skies one day, and snow the next.

The shrill sound of her cell phone ringing cut into the best part of her favorite song. Turning the radio down, she picked up her phone and answered. She touched the speakerphone button and waited. It was quiet for a moment and then the sound of a familiar voice filled the interior of her fully-restored 1951 Mercury.

"Did you miss me?" He offered no greeting or introduction.

"Vegas. Nice to hear from you." She was trying to sound aloof and nonchalant, "And where the fuck have you been?" and failed miserably.

"I'm sorry. I had to leave town for a while," he replied. "Had to take care of a few things and had to run out at the last minute. I didn't want to wake you up, and I didn't anticipate going this long without getting in touch with you. It's a long story, and one I promise to explain later. What are you doing tonight?"

No matter her level of irritation, the sound of his voice was perfectly disarming. Something along the lines of gravel wrapped in velvet, rugged and raspy but still silky smooth. Disgusted with herself, she rolled her eyes and then answered, "Onyx. To work, not for fun. Why? Are you going to come see me?" Her heart began to pound. She wanted to see him. Until this moment, she hadn't realized how much she missed him.

"I'll be there." She could hear the smile in his voice and grinned in return. She pushed her gas pedal to the floor, suddenly wanting to be at Onyx more than ever.

She arrived at work fifteen minutes earlier than she planned. The staff members were gathered by the bar for a pre-shift meeting. She tried to make her way into the back of the crowd as quietly as possible to avoid notice.

"Hey, Dez," the bar manager, Jack, greeted her with a warm smile.

He'd been a brilliant choice to run the bar in her absence. The whole staff loved him. He was strict about business but also extremely friendly; a quality her last few managers had severely lacked. He'd been there for about six months, and he fit right in with the family of existing employees from day one. The thing she loved most about having Jack around was his ability to deal with the shape-shifter community in a civilized manner and, more importantly, one that never resulted in her establishment needing repairs. If the average someone were to meet Jack on the street, they would never guess he turned into a tiger on occasion. At six-foot-one and roughly two hundred and thirty pounds, he just looked like any other guy who spent far too much time in the gym. His eyes didn't look wild either, a common trait of shifters. Instead, he had calm eyes: yellow-green close to the pupil, fading out to a gray-blue color. He always looked entirely at ease and she guessed it was part of the reason the staff got along with him so well.

No matter how laidback he seemed, Jack was a fiercely capable fighter in a bad situation. The recent increase in shifter clientele at Onyx was to be expected, but the violent outbursts which had come with it were not. Jack's ability to strong-arm even the biggest of shifters had created a reputation which prevented most incidents. Moreover, there was something about Jack which they could sense, maybe something about his tiger, and they knew better than to push their luck with him.

"Hi, guys." She waved and continued toward the staircase. She climbed the stairs to her office and glanced around once inside. She had purchased artwork to hang on the bare black walls, but the spots she had chosen remained vacant, the pieces on the floor leaning against the wall, still wrapped in protective paper from the gallery. She dropped her purse into the black and plum throne-style armchair in front of her desk and walked over to the large window, giving her a bird's-eye view of the club. The staff meeting was over and the employees were busily running through their normal routine, getting ready for the night to come. Onyx was a well-oiled machine.

She sat down at her desk and checked her messages before descending to walk the floor for the night. Observing the club was a safety measure she didn't normally take. She wanted to see for herself that Onyx was going to survive while she took some time off to travel. So far, she had nothing but confidence in her staffing choices. In addition to Jack, she had a good, hard-working group of people on her hands, all of whom seemed to care about the success of the club as much as she did. She hadn't told them yet that she was planning to leave for a while, but she assumed they had picked up a difference in the atmosphere by her more frequent presence. Although anxious thoughts haunted her anytime she thought about her upcoming departure, moments like this one told her that the club would survive without her for a little while.

But one more night of keeping an eye on things couldn't hurt. She turned and headed back downstairs.

Onyx was busy almost as soon as they opened the doors, and the time passed quickly. She ended up spending the first couple of hours helping out behind the bar. In a brief moment of peace between drink orders, she'd taken a second to scan the room and felt the small pinpricks of disappointment when she didn't see Vegas anywhere. They were still going to be open for a few more hours, so she did her best to extinguish the spark of annoyance developing in the back of her mind. After their phone call earlier, all her previous worries about why he'd left that night two weeks ago began to fall away. She couldn't see him standing her up again. Not after reaching out to her to say he'd be there. That just wasn't Vegas.

"Hey, Danni," she called to the slender bombshell of a bartender. She was the top earning bartender in the whole place and with good reason. Danni was stunning with her olive complexion, long black hair, chocolate brown eyes, and perfect veneers. She was pleasant to everyone and customers liked her, both men and women. Before her interview was even over, she and Dez had become fast friends. "I'm going to take a break up on the roof. When I come back down, I will run out back and grab some refills for you."

"Thanks, boss lady," Danni said, punctuating it with a flash of her pearly whites.

"No problem," Dez replied over her shoulder.

As she stepped out of the access door onto the flat

expanse of tarred roof, Deziree pulled a cigarette from the freshly opened pack, put it to her lips, and lit it. She could feel his presence as she took the first drag. She exhaled and smiled when she heard his voice behind her. She pushed it back and straightened her mouth into a hard line.

"Those are bad for you, you know." The sound of his voice sent a thrill running through her. When she spun around, he was standing just a few paces away.

"Hey, you." She gazed up at him and couldn't stop the smile from creeping across her lips again. Besides the fact that he was her best friend, she loved to look at him. He was by far the most beautiful creature she'd laid eyes on in her extraordinarily long life. He had the stereotypical bad boy image without all the pesky bad boy tendencies. Well, not ones that bothered her anyway. Tall, dark, and every bit of him was dangerous. He was just over six feet tall, the top of his smooth, shaved head towering above her. She idly pondered the number of razors he'd gone through over the centuries to keep that look. He had the perfectly chiseled appearance of a deadly hunter; which he was, in every way. Most people would have to spend hours in the gym every day for a body like his, but his undead status meant he didn't even have to try. He would look like that forever. Upon first glance, his eyes were the only tell-tale sign he was a vampire. Those irises—each a gleaming gold with a dark brown ring bordering the edge—were the only giveaway to the general public what he was. She, on the other hand, could *feel* it. She could feel the electricity crackle in the air whenever he was around. In more than four hundred years, she had never met someone as exciting as Vegas, and she'd wanted him from the moment they first met. But they had convinced themselves it was a bad idea, and standing here before him now, she couldn't remember why.

"Can I bum one off you?" He nodded toward the cigarettes.

"You would make a terrible spokesperson for anti-smoking public service announcements," she retorted with a snarky edge. As she fumbled with the pack of cigarettes, he stepped closer to her. Her nerves instantly hummed to life.

His predatory smirk and the slight glow of his eyes revealed his intentions, and in a blink, he closed what little remaining space there was between them. Reaching his hand around the back of her neck and tilting her head, he brought his lips crashing down to meet hers. Her head spun with euphoria. His scent washed away every negative thought she'd had about him in the last couple of weeks. When the kiss finally broke, it was not her doing. Taking a deep breath to calm herself, she opened her eyes to see his smile had grown wicked.

"You didn't answer me on the phone," he purred. "Did you miss me?"

"Well, with the harem of men I have at my disposal, I couldn't find the time to miss someone I only had a little fling with." She stepped back and added, "I mean, I didn't even get breakfast."

He dropped his gaze for a moment. "I deserve that." He nodded his agreement before continuing. "I really am sorry, Dez. For what it's worth, I didn't want to leave, I had to. It was a 9–1–1 and it was coven business. I didn't really have a choice in the matter. And I don't want you to get the wrong idea. I had a great time. I'm just hoping it won't be the last."

Deziree smiled. "I'm not mad. Not really. I mean, I was initially, but I figured something must have happened. A call or a text would have been nice. Something to let me know you weren't somewhere desiccating in an unmarked grave."

23

"Well," he said, his wicked grin firmly in place and his eyebrow cocked, "let me make it up to you."

"We'll see about that," she replied and her pulse quickened.

"I can hear your heart racing." Stepping forward, he leaned down and kissed her again. She found herself wishing she didn't have to go back down to the bar, but if she didn't, Danni was going to run out of liquor. He leaned his forehead on hers and whispered, "My place when you get out?"

"Sure," was her quick, breathy reply.

"I have a few things to take care of," he said quietly, "and then I'll meet you here around the time you guys usually lock up."

She nodded in response, and he turned, walked to the edge of the roof, and dropped off the side. After standing there for a few moments in a daze, she finished her cigarette, and headed back through the access door to grab the bottles she'd promised Danni.

CHAPTER FIVE

Michael

Michael had spent the previous two weeks feeling horrible about walking out that night. Deziree deserved better, and he knew it. When his presence was requested in Italy, he had no idea what he was getting into, and was forbidden to share any of the details of the case with anyone, including her. *Specifically* her. He had figured not calling and begging forgiveness when he returned would be easier than lying to her. He couldn't bring himself to lie to her, and he couldn't bear the repercussions if she ever found out he had. He knew he would have some making up to do when he got back. He just wasn't sure how much damage he'd done by leaving in the middle of the night without a word.

He expected Deziree would be furious with him, but she had forgiven him without any begging involved. He had every intention of explaining, regardless of her mild response. Holding back the truth about Italy would prove disastrous if she *did* come to find out. There had never been any secrets between them before and he wasn't about to begin keeping them now. Especially not with this.

Michael glanced at the clock on the kitchen wall. He

had just finished preparing dinner for the two of them, and it was almost time to go back over to Onyx and pick up Dez. Thinking of their informal date inspired happiness in him. He felt as though an enormous weight had been lifted off his shoulders now that he knew she didn't hate him. There was still a note of tension between them, but once he told her what happened, he was sure it would pass. The physical chemistry was still there, but Deziree had been so adamant years ago about their not starting a relationship. He wasn't sure if one night had changed her mind. His was made up. He knew what he wanted. The ball was in her court now.

CHAPTER SIX

Dez

Deziree was busy for the rest of the night, but it didn't keep her mind off Vegas. Her plan had never been to get involved with the vampire, but it was starting to appear the universe had other ideas for the pair.

The main reason she'd chosen a solitary life was her own immortality. It was a little difficult to explain to a potential suitor while they were growing old and wrinkly, her flawless alabaster skin would never be marred by the likes of crow's feet and age spots. Her long black hair would never turn a dignified shade of silver. Her impossibly blue eyes would never cloud with cataracts. Essentially, she would never look a day over twenty-five.

Living her life alone also lowered her chances of having to watch someone she loved wither and die. Over the centuries, she'd seen plenty of immortals fall in love, only to be left a mentally-destroyed mess when the object of their affections aged and inevitably passed on. Hell, Charlie was knowingly setting himself up for the very same fate.

Almost all immortal races were capable of deep

emotion, and a great many of them fell victim to it. Vampires, werewolves, shapeshifters, and every other race touched by magic all experienced love and grief on some level, some more intensely than others. She had vowed long ago she would never make the mistake of opening herself up to that kind of pain, and had done pretty well at keeping herself protected. She was half human, which meant she was extraordinarily susceptible to emotional connection. She had avoided forming bonds with anyone too easily, she had begun to think her half-demon DNA had over-powered those human tendencies. Sure, there were those she cared about but they were few and far between. Demonkind was the only race which was pure evil by nature, at least as far as she knew. Originally angelic souls, when they were sent to Hell, they were twisted and torn into something unrecognizable, their pure light snuffed and replaced by pure darkness. They were the originals, the purebloods, and the only emotions they're capable of were rage-fueled hatred and the occasional bout of pleasure born of someone else's pain. Not exactly the stuff happily ever afters were made of.

However, she felt something for Vegas that she'd never felt for anyone before. She loved him, but she had always loved him. He was practically her family. But that night had changed things. And then it was ripped out from under her the next morning when she woke to find herself alone. He had been nearly the sole occupant of her thoughts since; angry with him one minute even though she knew he would never have left like that without a good reason, and angry with herself the next for thinking the worst of him. It made for a shitty mood in the last couple of weeks. No matter what she did to steer her thoughts elsewhere, they never strayed far from him.

Neither of them had planned it, but maybe that was the point. Maybe two people were just destined to come together after spending so much of their lives in each other's company. Until the relatively recent public revelation that vampires and weres existed, they had bonded over the shared secret of immortality. Having to live in the shadows for so long seemed to drive an unspoken need to be honest with each other. There wasn't anything one kept from the other. She was a professional thief, and he was a mercenary for hire. Both jobs required a somewhat broken moral compass, so both knew they had no right to judge the other.

Michael's outlook on settling down with someone had always been much the same as her own: it was off-limits. He was a loner, even by vampire standards, and up until recently, their interactions had remained friendly, sexual tension-free zones. Now and then, conversation would be peppered with mild flirtation, but who didn't flirt? They spent their off time together, but things always remained friendly between them. Up until two weeks ago, they had spent a few hundred years successfully keeping it in their pants. They were confidants and companions in a life which would have otherwise been unbearably lonely. She thought that's how it would always be. She was apparently wrong.

The heat between them that night had been undeniable. The moment she'd seen him up on the roof earlier tonight, everything she felt that night came flooding back to her. Their one-night stand had clearly been more than a fling. She knew it was from her side, and she was fairly certain he felt the same way.

Last call came and went. Deziree and Danni scrambled to get the bar cleaned up in a mutual effort to get out of there as quickly as possible. She considered Danni one of her closest human friends. One of her only human friends, if she was being honest. Dez had brought her up to speed on the Vegas situation shortly after it happened, and upon being informed that he was going to be meeting her when they were done, Danni had taken it up as her personal mission to make sure Dez was out of there in record time.

When they declared victory over the messy bar, Danni grabbed her purse and in a quiet sing-song voice, she whispered, "Good luck," capping it off with a playful wink. Deziree laughed, shook her head, and ran upstairs to her office for her things. When she came back down, Jack and the rest of the crew had just finished for the night. Jack was the last to leave, and as he walked out the door, he called over his shoulder to say goodbye. She walked to the back and flipped all the light switches to the **OFF** position. She took one last look around to make sure nothing was left out of place. Satisfied, she turned and headed for the door.

Dez turned the key in the deadbolt lock.

"Hasn't anyone ever told you most girls are creeped out by guys who skulk in the shadows and watch people?" Deziree said before turning to smile up at him.

Vegas stepped away from the alley wall he'd been leaning against and into the light.

"Someone might have mentioned it once or twice," he replied. "Are you saying I give you the creeps?"

"Nah," she replied softly, "but I'm not most girls."

Vegas scoffed. "Tell me about it. Are you ready to go?"

"I am," she answered, and then asked, "Want to walk? It's finally dry out. I figured I can just leave my car here and get it later."

"Works for me."

The walk to his place wasn't far and she wanted to enjoy the night air. His brownstone penthouse was only a few blocks away from Onyx. However, the walk felt like an eternity as they strolled in a weird, slightly uncomfortable silence. The entire time she struggled with what she could or should say. He was the one who eventually spoke first.

"So how was work?"

"Not too bad. A couple of wolves got into a fight, but it was over pretty quickly. Having Jack around has definitely been beneficial. He hired a few guys from Lunacore for a little extra muscle parked around the room. The two guys they sent over are no joke. They're bigger than any were or shifter I've ever met, and neither of them seem to have a sense of humor. Needless to say, we don't chat. Ever."

Lunacore was a new security firm on the East coast. Based out of New York City, they were owned by an alpha werewolf, and they basically had a highly trained army of supernatural soldiers at their disposal. They were the new go-to if you had a security problem that couldn't be handled by the normal human means.

"Jack's a smart guy. I'm glad he got some extra help," he replied thoughtfully. "He's capable, no doubt, but one shifter is no match for an entire pack of angry wolves. What were they fighting over?"

"A girl; what else?" Dez shrugged. "She was drunk and willing, and they got into a territorial pissing contest over whom she'd be going home with. Apparently, there was some confusion regarding exactly who she was interested in. She was hanging all over both of them at different points throughout the night. They figured it out, and rather than getting pissed at her, they both came down with a case of testosterone poisoning. She was just an excuse to throw punches." She felt the awkwardness in the air break a little bit. This was the old them. This was the way they talked with each other prior to the night she'd come to refer to as The Incident when talking with Danni.

As they arrived at the brownstone, Vegas dug his keys out of his pocket, and unlocked his front door. When they got up to his penthouse, he opened the door and held it for her. She smiled. It was a sweet gesture. Familiar but different somehow.

"And here I thought chivalry was dead."

She walked in and set her bag on the hulking black leather couch in the center of his living room. No matter how many times she'd been here, she was always in awe when she saw his home. It was beautiful. Three of the four walls were bare brick, with the fourth wall of fully stocked, floor-to-ceiling bookcases. The living room and the kitchen were open, with a black marble island separating the two rooms. She'd always thought of his living room as being built for comfort. The large leather couch sat directly in front of a fireplace spacious enough for an average human to step into. Above the fireplace was a seldom-used flat-screen television. It was always kind of a mystery to her why he kept it. The only time it was ever used was when she came over. Vegas wasn't usually the couch potato type, but she'd gotten him to agree to a semi-regular ritual of kicking back and watching a movie together.

"It smells amazing in here," she said, inhaling the aroma of grilled chicken and a hint of garlic.

"I made us dinner," he replied as he closed the door behind them. He headed for the liquor cabinet tucked discreetly under the island.

"You cooked?" she asked, feigning shock. "What are we having?"

"Chicken alfredo." Nodding his head toward the fireplace, he asked, "Care to do the honors?"

She turned to the fireplace, closed her eyes, and took a deep breath. She rolled her neck, stretching the muscles, and then relaxed her shoulders. She opened her eyes again and whispered, "*Incendia*." Instantly, the logs in the hearth burst into flames as though someone had been carefully tending it for hours. She held her hand out to the fire and pushed down, taming the flames slightly.

"Someday, you're going to have to teach me how to do that," Vegas commented. "Speaking one word would be a lot easier than the newspaper and matches method. I don't have the patience for it."

"I've told you before," she replied, taking a seat on the couch, "you're a vampire, so you're already tied into the magicks. You just need to take the time to learn how to use them. It also happens to be one of the easiest spells to cast. It's one of the first most witches learn."

Vegas mixed their drinks and made their plates, then brought them into the living room on a tray. She tried to balance her reason against her emotions and still keep up with the conversation, trying her best not to look distracted. Her mind kept going back to The Incident. *Then there was the kiss on the roof of the Onyx ...*

"Well, that would blow this whole thing I have going," he remarked pointedly. "See, I invite you over for dinner and drinks, and you start the fire for me. Why mess with a good arrangement?"

He had to have thought about it, otherwise why would he have kissed me? They could go on avoiding the inevitable conversation, but if they didn't just get it out there, every future interaction between them would be affected by what had taken place that night.

"Very clever plan, my friend. Cheers." She raised her glass and took a sip of the pale pink Malibu Bay Breeze. The drink and dinner were both perfectly made as always. After a quiet moment, she asked, "So, where have you been for the last two weeks?" *Might as well just rip off the proverbial Band-Aid.*

"Venice, actually," he replied, staring into the warmth of the dancing orange flames, licks of blue appearing and disappearing. "I was called there by Cassandra. She needed me to investigate an occurrence."

"What do you mean, 'an occurrence'?"

Vegas was only called in to investigate for the covens when they needed to be discreet. Sometimes, cases were too dangerous for the human authorities to take on. They weren't prepared to deal with the vast array of strength and capabilities the supernatural community at large possessed. It's kind of hard to prepare for something when you don't even know it exists. So Cassandra would call Vegas in to handle it without the humans ever even knowing he was there. He was the best, and the high priestess trusted him implicitly.

"The new records keeper for the covens was murdered."

"Wow, that didn't take long." The records keeper position had only recently been filled due to the long overdue passing of her predecessor. Neither of them had met her, since the event to officially welcome her to the covens hadn't happened yet.

"No, it didn't. When Cassandra saw the condition of the girl's body, she called me immediately." He looked up from his plate and added, "She appears to have been burned from the inside out."

"Another fabrication for the record books?" she asked before stuffing another bite of alfredo in her mouth.

Vegas shook his head with doubt. "I don't know. If it was faked, I couldn't find anything to prove it."

While the majority of the supernatural community didn't mind public acknowledgment, it was decided the demons should remain in the shadows and nightmares. When they roamed the Earth, pureblood demons killed their victims by incineration from the inside out using their ability to conjure hellfire. It was their calling card, so to speak. The humans first called it witchcraft, then it was dubbed *spontaneous combustion*, but they were blissfully unaware there was nothing spontaneous about it. Eventually, a coven of witches discovered a way to drive the purebloods back down into Hell to remain locked there. The cases of spontaneous combustion since then had all been proven to be hoaxes.

After the purebloods were gone, the only signs of demon life on the human plane were the foot soldiers, the lesser demons created when a human soul was sent to Hell. They were a much less powerful, lower class of demons which would occasionally make an appearance. The human populace would spread accounts of the appearances as possession. When a foot soldier possessed a human, the victim would appear to be sick and start doing things which were completely out of character. Their behavior would progress, growing more violent and, in many cases, resulted in the victim hurting themselves. The possession would be enough to terrorize the victim, often leaving a mentally broken shell in their wake, and in a small percentage of cases, it would kill them. Unlike purebloods, foot soldiers were unable to command hellfire, but they caused enough trouble to be worrisome when they turned up.

It had been just over four hundred years since the last occurrence of a pureblood demon attack. Cassandra had been part of the group who located and stole the Sentinel Stone, the magical artifact which enabled the demons to cross over. The stone was made of brimstone taken from the Hell dimension itself. The witches from the Brujani Coven had taken a chance and opened themselves up to the dark arts. Through the use of blood magic, they were able to imbue the stone with an oath which sealed the gateways the demons had created. As long as the stone remained safe in the care of the Guardians, the purebloods would not be able to come through.

But if the demons ever gained access to it...

"Where is the stone?"

"Cassandra has soldiers working night and day to locate it as we speak. The Guardians aren't exactly a social lot, and no one's heard from them in years. Cassandra and the others are tracking them down to make sure the stone is exactly where it's supposed to be."

Deziree's mind was a mess of thoughts in every direction. One stood out. "Wait a second." She was suddenly confused and a little angry. "Why didn't Cassandra call me about this? Why the secrecy?"

Cassandra was a vampire and the priestess of the coven where Deziree had undergone her own training in witchcraft. Although she was born with natural ability, it still took a lot of time and practice to master it. She respected Cassandra more than almost anyone else and even saw her as a surrogate mother of sorts. Her own mother had committed suicide when Deziree was only hours old, leaving her with no memories of the woman. Cassandra had always been there to provide guidance in her mother's place.

"She wants to see what's what before she sends everyone, especially you, into an uproar," he explained. "So far, this attack is an isolated incident. We could be dealing with something totally unrelated."

"What about you? Do you think it was an attack?"

He took a slow breath and replied, "Well, I wasn't able to prove it was something else. It looked like a classic demon attack. If someone was trying to make it look authentic, I don't know how they did it, but they did a convincing job. I've seen and cleaned up plenty of these scenes, and I found nothing which gave it away as a fake. I waited around for over a week hoping to explain this away somehow, and I came up with nothing. Once I determined I could be of no further assistance, I came home."

Deziree turned her attention back to the fire, watching it sway and jerk as her mind poured over what she had just heard. *A pureblood demon attack.* She shook her head in disbelief. *If this is real, the covens will be facing something they never thought they'd see again in any of their lifetimes.* The last time purebloods walked the earth, they rained horrors down on the covens for years. The purebloods were a particularly nasty group with a tendency to murder for fun. No rhyme or reason. No motive. Just the desire for mayhem. If purebloods somehow found a way to reopen the gateways to the human realm, she had a sneaking suspicion they were in for the fight of their lives.

His voice broke her out of her thoughts. "Try not to worry about it until we know what the score is. In the meantime, the covens are on alert for possible danger and have taken the necessary precautions. Those women have proven on more than one occasion they can take care of themselves."

She knew he was right. A girl had died, yes, but death happens every day all over the world. One girl's death, although suspicious, did not mean the purebloods had found a way back. For all they knew, it was a case of a novice witch practicing a spell that was too far above her pay grade and it had backfired.

Pureblood demon attack or not, a coven member had been murdered. Finding her killer would be the Council's top priority. Until they knew for sure who or what had been responsible for her demise, there was no use getting worked up over something that may not even be a factor. She forced the negativity out of her head, determined not to let it ruin her night.

"Not that all this isn't important, but I wanted to talk to you about a temporary change of scenery. I wrapped up the Kingston job about a week ago, and I'm ready for a vacation. I want to get out of here. What do you say we go to Vegas, Vegas?"

She smiled at him with mock innocence and anticipation. Las Vegas was one of their favorite places to go for a getaway, and one of their many trips had led to his nickname. They had spent an entire night drinking and playing the blackjack tables. After losing a good deal of money to the casino, they ended up arm-in-arm, strolling through the bustling crowd on the Las Vegas Strip. Sitting by one of the large circular fountains outside Caesar's Palace, Michael had confessed his love for her. They were so drunk, in that moment she was convinced that he was just an overly happy drunk. She had explained to him it was the tequila talking, and when they woke up the next morning, the two laughed about the events of the night before. He claimed the confession was just an alcohol-induced emotional outburst and there really wasn't anything to it. That morning, she started calling him Vegas as a teasing gesture. Over time, the name stuck, and somewhere in the back of her mind, she had always wondered if there was more to his confession than he had admitted.

"I don't know," he replied apprehensively.

She held up one finger, she said, "Do you have any open contracts?"

"No," he admitted.

"Do you have any potential contracts you're aware of?" she asked, holding up a second finger.

"No," he replied, this time with a smile.

"Do you have any prior engagements you need to be in the city for?" she said, throwing up a third finger.

"No," he replied, his voice dropping low in obvious surrender.

"It's settled then," she answered, grinning from ear to ear. "You have your cell and your burner phones. If you're needed, you can hop the first flight to wherever you need to be. I'd even be happy to travel with you to keep you company. I wouldn't be in your way. It would all be very James Bond and Vesper Lynd." As soon as the words were out of her mouth, she realized what she'd said. She dropped her head and donned a nervous smile. "Seriously, put up your out-of-office and let's blow this joint."

"Dez, we really need to talk about this." By the look on his face, she knew he wasn't running, so she couldn't either.

"We probably should just get on with it," she responded with trepidation.

"Do you regret it?" he asked hesitantly.

She didn't think he knew what true regret even was. And for him to ask her if she felt it ... that was truly unexpected. But she had never regretted their night together; feared the results of it, maybe, but never regretted.

"Not exactly." She stood up and started to walk away from the couch. He caught her wrist, stopping her in her tracks. She looked down at his hand touching her skin and warmth flooded her body. He slid his hand down to hers and pulled her gently onto his lap so she was straddling him. He brushed a piece of her hair out of her face and tucked it behind her ear. It was a familiar gesture, but this time it was different. More intimate.

"Talk to me."

"We made a decision not to start anything once. I'm not sure if we should let one night together cloud our reasoning."

"What was the reasoning exactly?" he asked. "I'm having a hard time remembering any valid excuse for not getting together, aside from not wanting to ruin our friendship. We both know now it hasn't ruined anything."

"That was it. That was the only reason. I don't want to lose you if it all goes south."

"So let's make a deal," he countered. "If things don't work out for us as a couple, we just move past it and remain best friends. No harm, no foul. At least we will have tried instead of spending the rest of our lives wondering how good it *could* have been — wondering what we passed up."

"Is that possible? Could we really just get on with our lives like nothing happened?"

"Dez, I don't think we'll have to." She found it hard to not be swayed by the confidence in his voice. "I have spent the last two weeks thinking about this, and I honestly don't know what the hell we were waiting for. I don't know if there really are such things as soulmates, but I think we are probably as close as two people could get to being the definition of the term. I think we should give it a chance."

"Part of me wants to give it a shot," she admitted. "A big part of me. There's just this voice in the back of my mind screaming at me, telling me we would never be able to go back."

"Well," he replied softly, "hopefully we would never have to test that."

After taking a deep breath, he held up a finger.

"Do you have to worry about me shuffling off the mortal coil anytime soon?" His signature smirk was back. He was mocking her. A smile spread across her lips.

"Really?" she said, cocking an eyebrow at him. "You're quoting Shakespeare now? Wouldn't it be easier to just say you're not going to die?"

"You're deflecting, but fine," he replied. "Do you have to worry about me dying anytime soon?"

"No," she answered, knowing this would be the moment which would undoubtedly change everything. Not a drunken night of mind-blowing, Earth-shattering sex, but *this* moment.

Raising a second finger, he asked, "Do you have any reason to be dishonest and hide things from me?"

"No." Her voice was almost a whisper. Was this decision quite as easy as a handful of questions?

He raised a third finger. "Do you want to be with me?" His playful smile was replaced by hopeful anticipation dancing in his eyes.

Deziree thought for a moment. She'd already weighed all of the ups and downs of being with him. In fact, in all of her internal dialogue, attempting to talk herself out of what she knew she truly wanted deep down, she had yet to find a single valid reason for why they shouldn't be together. Everything about a relationship with Michael worked. It would be *easy*. Together, they made sense. There would be no surprises or secrets.

There really was nothing left to think about, nothing left to contemplate. As she stared into his golden eyes with their soft glow, she knew being with him was exactly what she wanted. She smiled and said, "Okay."

His joy mirrored hers. "I've been waiting to hear you say that." He lifted his head to kiss her, and when his lips met hers, she melted. As their kiss deepened, he wrapped his arms around her in a tight embrace. For the first time in all her years, she felt as though she was home.

CHAPTER SEVEN

Venice, Italy

Furio was standing in an alleyway to meet the man who'd hired him a few weeks before. He wasn't exactly sure who he should be looking for. The stranger had never shown his face in their previous meeting, their *only* meeting. The man hadn't asked him to do much either. He just wanted him to watch a building on the Grand Canal. He thought the request was a little odd, but when one was offered a job for that much cash, one didn't ask questions.

He grew restless standing there, bouncing from one foot to the other in nervous anticipation. He had been waiting for fifteen minutes, and no one had approached him. He sighed and leaned against the wall at the opening of the alleyway. He began debating whether he should stay or give up and leave, but was stopped by a voice from behind him.

"I apologize for my tardiness," the stranger said in perfect Italian, his raspy voice sending a chill down Furio's spine. "Do you have the information I requested?"

Furio turned to reply. He squinted but still couldn't see the man's face. The figure stood enveloped in shadow. He tilted head and replied, "Yes. I stayed for three days and then came back randomly for the following week, as you asked." He pulled a picture out of his pocket. "The first day, there were two men. The first arrived in the early evening. He wore a long black coat and carried an expensive-looking cane. He was there for a long while and then left. He wasn't gone for very long when a second man arrived. He stayed briefly and then left. He looked quite upset when he left. The way he moved ... "

"The way he moved?" The stranger's voice was quiet as he asked the question.

"Yes," Furio replied hesitantly. "He moved faster than anyone I have ever seen. He looked normal, but no man can move that fast."

"What else?"

Furio thought the stranger's lack of interest off-putting. For his part, he was quite rattled at seeing a man move that way. "The evening of the third day," he continued, "a woman arrived. She was there for a few hours and then left. The next day, the bald man you told me to expect showed up." He held out the paper, and the stranger took it. "He was there every time I came by."

"Is there anything else?"

Furio shook his head. "No, that was all," he said, "If you need anything else done, you know where to find me." The investigator turned to leave but the stranger stopped him.

"There is one more thing I'd like to know. Did you tell anyone about our arrangement?"

Furio shook his head. "No, sir. No one knows we ever even spoke. Just like you said."

"Thank you. Your services will no longer be required." The stranger stepped out of the shadows, revealing his face to the rattled man for the first time. Furio's eyes widened in horror at the sight of him.

43

Gray skin stretched over severe cheekbones. Glassy black eyes shone in the scarce light and razor-sharp teeth glinted in a growing grin. No, he wasn't a man at all. The creature was terrifying. The being flashed a cruel smile and an icy chill ran through Furio's body as recognition dawned. *The man with the long, black coat and the cane.* The cold was abruptly followed by an intense heat and searing pain deep inside his abdomen, then swiftly flowed through his entire body. As he let loose a blood-curdling scream, the stranger reached out with lightning speed and in one smooth motion, snapped Furio's neck, leaving his head dangling at an unnatural angle as the flames erupted from his lifeless body.

※

The stranger pulled a cell phone out of his coat pocket. He dialed a number and as the line rang, he wiped his hands clean. When the person on the other end picked up and greeted him, he skipped the pleasantries and got right to the point. "One of the parasites was there. Not the one we were already aware of. I'm not sure how much this one would know. I think it best to accelerate our schedule." He hung up the phone without speaking another word or bothering to wait for a response. He smiled to himself and strolled out into the night never thinking of the dead man again.

CHAPTER EIGHT

Dez

Deziree woke up the next morning in a daze. And a whole lot of pain. As soon as she opened her eyes, she wished immortality included immunity from hangovers. Much to her dismay, it did not. Every joint in her body ached, a death metal band with a blown sound system had set up shop in her head, and she was pretty sure she could drink an entire swimming pool she was so thirsty. With great effort, she rolled over and realized she was alone — again. An unsettling sense of déjà vu washed over her, and if she wasn't positive it would hurt like hell, she would have rolled her eyes.

She sat up, put her feet on the cold wood floor, and hauled herself out of the bed. She grabbed a button up shirt belonging to Vegas and slipped it on. When she made her way to the kitchen, she found Vegas at the island with a mug and a laptop. He looked up and smiled.

"Good afternoon. I didn't want to wake you. I wasn't sure how tired you were going to be. Do you want anything for lunch?"

"Lunch?" With confusion, Deziree glanced at the clock

on the kitchen wall. It was just after one o'clock. "Oh, I thought it was a lot earlier than that. Actually, I'm not really hungry. I'm a teeny, tiny bit hungover."

"Yeah, me too. And this stuff," Vegas said as he held up his glass and looked into it, "tastes like liquid death, which is not helping matters." The thick red substance swirling around in the glass was tempero, a concoction Cassandra had created to help curb a vampire's appetite for blood. Tempero wouldn't take away the need completely. However, it allowed a vampire the ability to go for months at a time between feedings, giving them plenty of time to seek a willing donor or purchase a supply from the local blood bank. The drink wasn't commonly used in the vampire community, but Cassandra had made it readily available to those who chose to live a tamer lifestyle, and Vegas had been one of the first to take her up on it.

Although Vegas didn't choose to become a vampire, he had accepted what he was, and made the best of his supernatural abilities. His mother, a natural-born witch, allowed the covens to change both him and his brother to aid in the war against the demons. It was tough for both of them at first, getting used to the blood cravings, but he managed, and never once did he apologize for what he was. In reality, there was no reason to. A vampire's nature was to be a predator, and he found a niche in the world which allowed him to be just that. The downside to his job was finding a suitable form of nourishment when on a fourteen hour flight to the opposite side of the globe. Without the assistance of tempero, his body would require him to feed at least twice a day. If he didn't have tempero, and went too long without feeding, he would end up in a blood fever. A blood fever has only one result: death for anyone in the immediate vicinity of the vampire caught up in the whirlwind of blind rage and hunger. One glass of the viscous, foul-smelling red liquid every day ensured he wouldn't slip into a mid-flight feeding frenzy, killing all the occupants of whatever airbus he happened to be on.

Dez wasn't clear on the details because it was before her time, but as she understood it, Cassandra had set on her quest to create tempero for the sole purpose of using white magic. Vampires and witches usually didn't mix because dark magics were fueled by blood. Adding blood to a simple spell like, for example, the one used to light a candle, and a witch could start a fire storm which would be close to impossible to get under control. Cassandra, with her beautiful heart and good spirit, did not want to be limited in what she could do by the fact that she had a set of fangs.

"Yeah," she answered with a smile, "if you had the faintest idea of the long list of nasty ingredients that go into that little bottle of ick, you'd be draining the next human who walks by rather than accepting the alternative."

"Ignorance is bliss." He sighed as he tipped his glass and emptied it in one swallow. As soon as he finished, he caught her watching him. After a moment of searching her eyes, not completely positive of what she was thinking, he finally spoke up. "Now that you've had a chance to get some sleep and," he smiled, "we don't have our tongues in each other's mouths, I need to ask. Are you sure about this? Don't get me wrong, I'm on board, and I hope you are too, but sitting here drinking this shit is a heavy reminder of our differences."

"*Michael. Tremayne*," she scolded, and then launched a verbal assault as she poured and dressed her coffee. "That is the dumbest thing you could possibly have come up with. I'm the bastard child of a pureblood demon and the witch he raped, was raised by a vampire, then trained as a witch myself. I'm not bothered by those of the *toothy* persuasion, you already know that. So if that's all you've got, yes, I'm sure about this. It's not like anything much about us will really change. The frequency with which I see you naked, and warm, fuzzy feelings we are no longer pretending to ignore. That's pretty much it." With a sigh, she sank into the chair opposite him and sipped her coffee. She glared at him expectantly over the lip of her coffee mug and waited for his response.

He had listened patiently to her rant. She supposed he was accustomed to speeches of that kind, ranting being a common habit of hers. A smile played at the edges of his mouth, giving her the reassurance they were okay. The glowing in his eyes when she mentioned the word *naked* was also a good indication.

"Why?" she asked sarcastically. "Do you suddenly have something against hot half-demons?"

"You know it." His deadpan response wasn't convincing anyone. "Wretched beings. They're hideous, covered in boils, and the smell. It's gross. I have no idea how you go out in public every day."

"Really good concealer," she replied without missing a beat.

"Look, I had to ask." He was quiet for a moment before he continued. "I want you to know I'm not going anywhere. I want this, even if you do fuck up my freshly pressed shirts." He gave her a wink. It felt good to hear, even if she no longer had any doubts or misgivings about the road they were about to venture down. All of the time she spent second guessing and being angry with him now seemed wasted. It all seemed incredibly silly to her. She put it out of her mind, determined to focus on more positive things.

Deziree leaned her elbows on the countertop and smiled maniacally. "So when do we book our tickets?"

"Well," he started hesitantly, "I got a call this morning that may delay our travel plans by a day or two. It appears

Lucas has been roaming the city for the last week and a half now and plans to stop by."

Deziree squealed excitedly. "Really? That's random. I haven't seen your brother in years."

"Me either."

"I wonder what kind of trouble he's in. Why didn't he just come here? Or at least go to Onyx? Anyone there could have told him where you were, including yours truly. Seems a little dumb to just wander around the city aimlessly."

"When he couldn't get a hold of me, he assumed we were off somewhere together."

Dez nodded. It's not like it was an outlandish assumption for someone to make. She and Vegas had been to all corners of the earth together over the years.

"Fair enough." She waved her hand over her mug and whispered an incantation. The spoon began to dance slowly around the mug, stirring her coffee. "Well, it'll be fun to see him."

"Yeah," Vegas rolled his eyes, "a real blast. As for what he's been up to, I think that has something to do with why he's here. You've seen Lucas just as much as I have. We don't hang out. His desire to pay us a visit is highly suspect."

Lucas Tremayne was a veritable walking magnet for trouble, the kind of trouble with peroxide-blonde hair and fake D cups. He had a widespread reputation for bedding any woman who would have him, whether she was spoken for or not. The last time they had seen each other, he was facing a sentence of the final death for sleeping with another vampire's wife. The girl had represented one of the few offenses in vampire law which warrants final death, and he just couldn't keep his hand out of the cookie jar. Upon being caught, Lucas had begged Vegas, once again, to bail him out. It required the pulling of some very expensive strings, but in the end, Lucas was freed and cleared of all charges. The husband had miraculously decided the sins of his wife were forgivable after all, proving once again that everyone has a price.

For all of his promiscuous behavior, Lucas had always respected Deziree, never once making a pass at her. Their banter was always playful but never anything shocking or distasteful. As much as she was looking forward to seeing him, she also knew Vegas was right. An impromptu visit from the younger Tremayne usually meant he'd buried himself in some sort of mess.

"I wonder what it is this time." She took another sip off of her coffee and idly thumbed at the mug's smooth handle as she pondered over the possibilities.

"I'm not sure," he replied, "but he said it was urgent. He's supposed to be here in about an hour, which means you and I have that long to get our trip booked." He smiled, stood up and gestured for her to sit down in front of his laptop. "Figure out which hotel you want to stay at, and I will take care of the rest. While you do that, I'll get another pot of coffee made."

Deziree moved to the other side of the island, sat down, and opened up the internet browser. She had chosen Las Vegas as their vacation spot because of the city's nightlife. No matter what one wanted to do to pass the time, there was always a twenty-four hour place ready and waiting. Contrary to the storybook tales, vampires could easily go out in daylight. However, it *was* more comfortable for them to go out at night. With their extremely heightened eyesight, sunlight tended to be an irritant. When she decided she wanted to go on a vacation, she wanted to go someplace warm, and even in the darkest hours, and a Las Vegas night felt like a warm summer's day.

She ended up choosing the Luxor Casino. She had

been to the city a number of times, but had never stayed there. Since she wanted to see something new, the modernized pyramid seemed like a good choice. The ancient Egyptian-themed decor sounded like an intriguing atmosphere, and the hotel was located within walking distance of the other attractions she wanted to visit. With that settled, Vegas booked a first-class flight and even got a suite, which looked more like a luxury apartment than a hotel room.

She was on the phone with Jack informing him she'd be taking a few weeks off when the doorbell rang. Knowing it was his brother, Vegas buzzed him in and stepped out into the hallway to greet him. Deziree nursed her coffee and thought about how much things had changed overnight. Feelings of apprehension began to creep into her mind again, and she immediately stopped herself. She made the right choice with Vegas, she knew that, but after all the time they had known each other, old habits were proving hard to break. She was comfortable living a somewhat solitary life. After so long, it came naturally to her. There would be adjustments, sure, but he was probably right. They wouldn't be as drastic as she feared. She smiled. *Just roll with it, Davanzati. What have you got to lose?*

She was just hanging up her phone when Vegas walked in, trailed by his brother. Lucas looked at her, a mischievous grin spread across his face. His golden irises twinkled and just a hint of glow began to show.

"Deziree," he purred in greeting, his eyes panning down her body. Deziree remembered she was still only wearing Vegas's button-up shirt. She smiled and said "One minute," stood up, and ran for the bedroom. She shut the door behind her, and after fishing through her duffel bag, she hurriedly threw on a pair of sweatpants and a t-shirt. She could hear the men having a conversation in the living room, their voices muffled behind the closed door. Once she was decent, she made her way back out to join them.

"Sorry about that."

"No apologies necessary," Lucas replied with a sly smile. "I'd say it's been a long time since a woman has greeted me in such a way but, well, that would be a lie. How have you been, Dez?"

He walked over, took her hand, and kissed the back of it. It was so gentlemanly, she had to remind herself he was anything but. She rolled her eyes and looked up into his face. Something in his smile wasn't quite right. If it were necessary for a vampire to sleep, she would have guessed he was suffering from severe exhaustion by the way his smile didn't quite make it to his eyes.

"Good," she replied. "How about you, Lucas? Is it an angry husband or a scorned woman hot on your trail that has you gracing us with your presence?"

He ran a hand through his short black hair and sat down on the couch. She was always amazed seeing the two brothers side by side. They looked absolutely nothing alike. Vegas was solid, built more like a boxer with toned bulk to spare. Lucas had an Olympic swimmer's body, slender but athletic.

His handsome face turned serious, pain haunting his eyes. "I wish it were as simple as all that. I can say with a completely clear conscience that I did nothing wrong." He huffed. "You're probably going to find this relatively hard to believe, but I fell in love."

"Wow, I did not see that coming," she replied.

"And she was a human. A witch to be more precise. Michael, I believe you met her approximately two weeks ago. Her name was Natalia."

"Was?" Dez asked, feeling like she was missing a piece of the puzzle.

"The burn victim ..." Vegas remarked with gravity.

Lucas had been involved with the burn victim in Venice. "Please, Lucas, tell me you had nothing to do with that."

"Of course I didn't!" Lucas exclaimed. "I fell for someone for the first time ever and you think I could do something like that to her? You know me better than that. I may be a bit of a scoundrel, but I'm not a killer. We had plans, she and I. Nothing grand. We just wanted to be together. She knew what I was, knew what it meant to be with me, and accepted me anyway." Lucas stood up from the couch and paced back and forth through the room. "I saw him. I saw the thing that killed her. It wasn't human." He stopped moving and looked Vegas in the eye. "It was a pureblood. His aura was black as tar."

"You're sure?" Vegas asked. Lucas sat down opposite him at the island counter and leaned in, his words urgent and full of conviction.

"I'd swear my life on it. Your life, her life. It was a pureblood, no mistake. And even from the significant distance between us, I could feel the power radiating from him. Whoever he is, he's old, and he's got a lot of juice. The last time I felt anything like it was before the covens were able to close the gateways."

"I don't understand. How would a pureblood have made it onto our plane?"

"Good question. I've been asking myself the same thing and I've got nothing. That's why I came to you guys. I know what I saw, what I felt. They can play dress-up and try to make themselves look human all they want, but no one can disguise their aura. Even serial killers don't have pure black auras. There is always a glint of something else there, glimmers of humanity. This thing had no humanity in it. I went back the next night, when I was sure the coast was clear, and I saw the body. Michael, you saw her with your own eyes. There is no doubt in my mind and there shouldn't be any in yours. A pureblood demon murdered the only girl I've ever loved." His normally carefree face was riddled with pain, the kind of pain only caused by the loss of a loved one. In that look, all of their greatest fears were realized.

"Looks like our trip is out of the question for the time being," Vegas said. "We'll have to come up with a plan." Deziree only felt a momentary twinge of disappointment. She knew if they didn't find and stop this thing, there wouldn't be a Las Vegas to go to.

"We need to call Cass immediately," Deziree said. "The covens need to prepare. If a pureblood has the stone, we're fucked." Vegas nodded in agreement and pulled out his cell phone. He stepped out to make the call. She glanced at Lucas, who was now sitting back in his chair. He looked hopeless and lost.

"Hey," she said softly, sitting down next to him. She took his hand in hers and rubbed the back of it gently. "I'm so sorry about your girlfriend."

His eyes welled with tears. "Thanks," he croaked.

"I don't think I've ever seen you cry before," she said. "It looks like falling in love has changed you."

"It has," he agreed. "Natalia was beautiful and amazing and ..." He sniffed hard, wiping his eyes. "There aren't any words in human languages which can really describe who she was. I couldn't avoid being changed by her. I feel lucky to have had her in my life, even if only for a short while. And if I just keep telling myself that, one day I'll believe it." They sat quietly until he achieved some semblance of composure. "It's changed you too, you know. Both of you."

"What?" she asked.

"You and Michael. I'm glad you both finally pulled your heads out of your asses and saw what was right in front of you. Everybody else saw it a long time ago." He smiled and punctuated the statement with a wink.

"Yeah," she replied, "well, I don't think either of us was ready to see it until now. You could be right though."

"I *could* be right?" he teased. "You two are made for each other. I have never met two people who are so alike. You even have the same affinity for violence and guns." With a smile, he added, "Remind me to get you matching Desert Eagles as your wedding gift."

Dez shook her head and laughed. "No one said anything about nuptials."

Vegas came out of the bedroom and it was immediately obvious he was all business.

"Cassandra just heard back from the team who was sent to track down the Guardians," he said. "They're dead, all five of them. All found in the same condition as Natalia."

"That's it then," Dez said, standing up. It was her turn to pace the room. "Somehow the demons got their paws on the stone and they're here."

"We don't know that it's more than one," Vegas argued.

"No, but that's still one too many. They have the stone. Even if it is just one, that's only going to last for so long."

"I think we need to go to Venice," Vegas replied. "We'll call the covens for an emergency meeting and see how they want to proceed. We need to find out how much manpower we have. Right now, we only know of one pureblood on this plane, but if it has the stone, odds are pretty good it's planning to use it to open the gateways and let all his buddies through. Lucas, you're more than welcome to stay here if you'd like."

"The fuck I am," he retorted with exasperation. "I'm not staying here alone. If you two are going to Venice, then I'm going too, if only for the fraction of a chance I might be the one to cut the head off the piece of shit who took Natalia from me."

CHAPTER NINE

Michael

A few hours later, the three of them were on an international flight to Venice, Italy. Before they left, both Michael and Lucas took an extra dose of tempero. The flight shouldn't have been long enough to put them at a high risk for cravings, but they weren't willing to take any chances. Michael gazed out the airplane window at the inky black of the night sky. Deziree shifted in her sleep and he turned to her to look at her. A piece of her raven hair was dangling down over her face and he swept it back, careful not to wake her. Despite his efforts, her eyes fluttered open and she smiled at him.

"Hey, where are we?" Her voice was groggy as she rubbed the sleep from her eyes. She'd been out for a little while, yet somehow still looked incredible.

"Somewhere over the Atlantic. You haven't been asleep for very long." He looked back out the window, his mind still turning. After a few minutes of silent contemplation, he finally spoke again. "Dez, how did they get here?" He turned his attention to her. "Into our dimension, I mean. How did they get *here*? Without the stone, they aren't supposed to be able to cross either way, and yet we have a pureblood on our hands."

"He had to have had help," she answered. "Someone summoned him, it's the only possible explanation. Whoever the culprit is would have to be a powerful practitioner with an extensive knowledge of blood magic. That kind of conjuring couldn't be done by just anyone."

"That narrows down the list of players by quite a lot," he said. "Unfortunately, that list includes people we know."

There weren't many witches left practicing blood magic. The practice was widely viewed by the covens as dirty and, more importantly, dangerous. The majority of blood magic was based in the dark arts and therefore frowned upon. There was no ban against it in their world, but very few openly admitted to dabbling. At the top of that list were individuals they knew, and in some cases, people they were close with.

"I hope not," she replied. "Who knows, maybe there's someone who just recently has come into their power and we don't know about it. It wouldn't be the first time a witch stayed under the radar." He gave her an incredulous look. She took a deep, cleansing breath, leaned her head back on the seat and closed her eyes. "It's worth hoping for," she added before slipping back into her slumber.

❦

The following night, the Council of Covens was meeting at the Brujani estate, the base of operations for a few centuries now. Michael and Deziree chose to attend the meeting, leaving Lucas to wait at the hotel. From where he was leaning against the wall, Michael glanced around the large meeting hall. The Council members had assembled quickly and now filled the seats at the long cherry wood table. They talked busily amongst themselves, no doubt speculating about why they were called together.

"I didn't expect them to get here so quick," Deziree said as she walked up and leaned against the wall next to him.

"Most of them were just a plane ride away," he explained. "Cassandra let them know there was an urgent situation as soon as we realized the stone was in jeopardy. She hasn't told them what the situation is yet. It's been so long since they've had to come together, they were probably looking forward to the trip."

"You think they'll freak out?"

"Absolutely."

The Council of Covens consisted of the most senior member of each coven from around the world. In all, there were eight covens, each with a body of witches and a body of vampires. Each body had a representative at the table. The only coven without a representative for both was the Brujani coven. That's where Cassandra came in. Being both a witch and a vampire, she served as the voice for both.

Michael stepped away from the wall and turned to Deziree, pretending to lean in and kiss her cheek. "Don't forget what we discussed in the hotel room. No matter what is said here, we can't let our suspicions show, and don't let anyone know Lucas witnessed the demon. The only way we are going to find out if one of our people is responsible is if we keep quiet and let them think they've gotten away with it," he whispered.

Cassandra entered the room. All chatter amongst the Council members ceased, and the ones who were standing rushed to their seats. Cassandra Giordano was seen as the Council's unofficial leader. The other members treated her with reverence and sought her guidance when it was needed. The silence claiming the air upon her arrival was a common occurrence whenever she entered a room.

Cassandra cleared her throat and addressed the group, her voice soft and sultry. "Thank you all for your patience. Once everyone is settled, we'll begin." When Cassandra was done speaking, she spotted Deziree. Smiling, she approached the couple and took Deziree's hand in hers. "Child, it's been too long. I wish it were under better circumstances, but I can't tell you how happy I am to see you." Michael watched the two reunite. When two beings knew each other as well and for as long as Cassandra and Dez, silence was often the most efficient ambassador of joy.

"Michael," she greeted him, "it's good to see you as well. I was hoping we wouldn't have to see each other again so soon, but it seems the universe has other plans for us." She eyed them curiously for a moment. "I'm detecting a new connection between the two of you." She glared back and forth between them with a crooked smile on her face. Michael didn't know what to say. He'd avoided talking about the developments in his and Deziree's relationship when he'd been there on investigation. Cassandra laughed and put her arms around both their shoulders. "Come now, children! Did you really think I would be upset by this? On the contrary, I believe it is long overdue! I'm glad you are both here. I'm sure there will be a lot of questions and many long answers to be given for them." Cassandra surveyed the room, seeking out someone specific. She caught eyes with a younger Italian vampire and waved him over.

"Carlo, would you do me a favor and get a small table and some chairs for Michael and Deziree? Also, please have the kitchen put together a plate of refreshments for them." Cassandra rounded on the two of them and smiled again. "Enjoy." With that, she turned and glided to her seat at the far end of the table.

Carlo bustled about, getting their table and chairs set up as the Council members took their seats. The thin, dark-haired vampire whispered his assurance that their beverages and something sweet from the kitchen would be brought out to them right away.

The whole room hushed again and everyone waited for Cassandra to speak. Michael studied the faces of all those in attendance. He had no idea who would be working with the demons and was at a total loss for theories. He couldn't even understand why a vampire or a witch would work with the purebloods. They had nothing to gain and everything to lose by offering a hand to help the demons open the gateway. Michael knew there had to be more to it, he just didn't know what.

"Greetings, everyone," Cassandra announced. "Let's call this meeting to order, shall we?" She eased into her seat and the entire room's attention was on her.

"This is what we know," she began, a somber note breaking into her voice. "Just over two weeks ago, our new records keeper was brutally tortured. After being tortured, she was murdered, incinerated from within by means of hellfire, as far as we can tell."

Gasps echoed around the room as the weight of her words took hold, after which there was an eruption of murmuring.

She stood. "Ladies and gentleman, please." When they quieted, she continued speaking. She took her time, choosing her words carefully. "As unfortunate as Natalia's passing is, I genuinely wish I could say it was the worst of what I have to report this evening." The room's attention was returned to her and she eased back down into her seat. "Immediately following Natalia's murder, the Guardians were also murdered in the same manner. The stone is missing. As I am sure you have all gathered, it would appear we have a pureblood demon in our realm, the first of its kind since the sealing of the gateway, and no idea how it got here. I have brought you together tonight so we may devise a strategy. There's only one use for the stone, and that is to reopen the gateway to the Hell dimension. We are at a distinct disadvantage and must come up with a plan."

"But what *can* we do?" asked Kade, the vampire leader of the New York-based Walker coven and one of Michael's best friends. "The last time we sealed the gateway, we used a spell with the help of the stone. The stone would have to be found and the spell would have to be recreated."

"Do you have any idea where the stone or this demon are now?" This time it was Klaudia who spoke, the leader of the Russian Semerikov coven.

"At this time, we have no leads. Everyone who has faced off with the demon has turned up dead. I have spread the word out to many of my people across Italy and the surrounding countries in my territory. One reason for holding this meeting is to count our resources. Who can you spare to help track down the demon? Should we manage to find the creature before it does any more real damage, our best course of action would be to destroy both it and the stone. This is not a burden I want our future generations to bear. With that said, I am going to go around the table to each coven. Decide if your coven will stand down or fight with us. Witch covens, you are needed to recreate the spell we used to seal the gateways the last time. We need to be prepared for all possible scenarios."

Michael watched the ethereal lady move from member to member. All of the vampire covens agreed to stand with the council and each made a promise of manpower for the effort. All but one of the witch covens agreed to participate in the recreation of the spell. The Lee coven, whose territory spanned all of Australia and New Zealand, had a member who had dabbled in blood magic as a girl and she became addicted. She couldn't risk being exposed to it again. They did offer their services in other ways by procuring and transporting rare ingredients, and also arranging travel and lodging for witches who would have to fly in to lend their aid. By the end, everyone had decided to lend support. No one could afford not to.

"Thank you all," Cassandra said, looking around the table at the worried faces. "We have quite a bit of work ahead of us, I'm afraid. Please, make yourselves at home here. There is plenty of space throughout the manor. If you require a quiet room to contact your coven members, Carlo can arrange to help you with that." She paused and took a weighted breath. "We will stop this. We will. I need you all to have faith. Have faith in each other and our combined abilities. We *will* stop it." The entire table visibly relaxed and light conversation commenced.

CHAPTER TEN

Deziree

As she watched the coven members break off into conversation, Deziree could only keep her mouth shut for so long.

"Where is the gateway?" Her question commanded everyone's attention, including Cassandra's. "Why don't we hold a sting operation and head him off at the pass? If we watch the gateway site, we can stop him from opening it."

"That would be a wonderful plan if there were only one possible gateway site," Kade answered. Deziree watched a look of mild amusement cross his face.

"Well, exactly how many are there?" she probed. This time it was Vegas who answered.

"No one really knows. The popular theory is that the gateway sites are the locations on the Earth where ley lines intersect. The magical hotspots fueled the spell in both directions to open a gateway and to close it. They'd just have to pick one. Wherever the gateway is opened must be a spot where the veil between the spirit realms and our own are at their thinnest, and the ley lines are literally a roadmap with hundreds, maybe thousands, of locations that would work. The best chance we have of stopping all of this is to track the pureblood down and end it." Then he turned and addressed the Council members. "I agree with Cassandra. We should destroy the stone once the demon is dispatched. This never should have happened, never should have been *allowed* to happen. Had the stone been destroyed when we closed the last gateway, the records keeper and the Guardians would still be alive today."

Deziree knew what Vegas was doing. He was well aware there was only one way to destroy the Sentinel Stone: to burn it with hellfire. No demon would voluntarily destroy the stone. That left the only option being a trip through an open gateway into the depths of the hell dimension, and no one present was eager to make the journey. Closing the gateway permanently meant closing off any means of return. Vegas was trying to flush out the party responsible by proposing something he knew they would be directly opposed to. If anyone spoke against the suggestion, they were likely involved.

She glanced around the room, watching the faces of everyone around the table. Everyone in the room was looking to each other and silently nodding their heads in agreement. It was Cassandra who finally broke the silence.

"I cannot say I am happy about the suggestion to sacrifice one of our own," she stated as she stared down at the center of the table. She took a deep breath as she raised her eyes to address the Council and continued. "However, I also cannot deny the gravity of the situation or the lack of alternative options. If they were able to return once, it will almost certainly happen again, and we cannot have that. Too much life has been taken already. First, let's focus on stopping the pureblood. Once the immediate danger has been brought to a conclusion, we will convene again to discuss the destruction of the stone. Are we all agreed?"

Well, there went that theory. Nothing. No one shifted uncomfortably under the weight of their guilt. It was back to square one.

CHAPTER ELEVEN

Lucas

"Well?" Lucas was on his feet the minute they walked through the door of the lavish hotel suite.

"Nothing," Dez responded. "I will let him fill you in on everything. I need to go take a shower or drown myself. I haven't decided yet." She turned and left the room without another word.

Lucas tried to calm himself and exercise some patience. He'd always been the relaxed sort, but when Natalia died, something in him broke. He'd spent the last two weeks as a nervous wreck. He'd done his best to cover it when he finally went to see Michael and Deziree, but his control was slipping. Being back in Venice – smelling the air, seeing the streets – brought him right back to the moment he first saw Natalia's charred remains. *His* Natalia.

Michael had been going on about the meeting, when he noticed Lucas was distracted. "Hey, are you alright?"

He hadn't realized he was so lost in his own head and had no idea what he had missed. "I'm far from alright. I can't stop thinking about her. All I want to do is choke the life out of the thing who did this."

"Don't worry, man. We *will* figure this out," Michael reassured him. "The one thing we can count on is that all beings make mistakes. This pureblood is no exception."

"I hope you're right." Lucas sat up straight, rubbed his face, and then gave his brother all of his attention. "It's just that being here is like pouring salt in the wound. I'm just finding it hard to focus." The only way he was going to get his vengeance was if his head was in the game. He would have eons to mourn his loss when this was all over. "Start over. I promise I'm listening this time," he said, forcing a smile.

CHAPTER TWELVE

Deziree

Deziree quietly shut the door behind her. The master bedroom of the suite was so silent that the click of the latch snapping into place sounded like a handgun blast in her ears. She went into the luxurious bathroom and ran the water until it was piping hot.

Steam filled the air. She retrieved a few towels from the linen closet and tossed them on the counter. She stripped off her clothes, leaving them in a messy pile on the floor.

Stepping inside the shower, Deziree let the hot spray envelope her. She closed her eyes, dunked her head under the steady stream, and let it wash all of her worries away. Bad things were on the horizon, she could feel it instinctively. The worst part of the situation was not knowing exactly what those bad things were. She hadn't become a successful jewel thief by luck. Without the use of meticulously laid out plans, everything would fall apart. In this situation, getting ahead of the carnage was key.

Deziree soaked her hair, scrubbing her tense scalp with her fingertips. Soon, the hot water was working its magic. She visualized the tension falling away from her body in waves. Leaning her head against the warm tile wall, she felt relaxed for the first time in three days.

She wasn't sure how long she'd been standing there blocking the world out before she heard the glass shower door quietly slide open. A smile crept across her face but she didn't open her eyes. The current of energy which rolled over her body told her everything she needed to know of who her intruder was.

One of Vegas's arms crept around her waist as his other hand brushed her wet hair aside. He nuzzled his face in the crook of her neck, and then made a trail of light kisses from her shoulder up to the sensitive spot right behind her ear. She wondered how such a small action could cause such an immense wave of arousal, and as he pressed his body against hers, baser instincts took over.

She turned to face him. He took the opportunity to run his hands up her sides and along her arms to her wrists. With authority, he pinned them against the warm tile above her head. She looked up into his half-lidded eyes. The mellow gold took on a hungry glow. He teased the side of her neck with his tongue. Deziree shut her eyes and the rest of the world melted away. It was just her, Vegas, and the rush of water. Nothing else existed.

He kissed the delicate curve of her jaw until finally his mouth claimed hers. Guiding her arms down over his head and around his neck, he didn't pull away from the kiss. The longer they stood locked in the embrace, the louder and heavier their breathing became. The more intense the kiss became, the faster her heart raced. Heat flooded every part of her body and she moaned, digging her fingernails into his back. His body's response was instantaneous.

She felt his sharp fangs against the side of her tongue and the sensation forced her back to her wits. She broke away, her breath coming in ragged pants. His eyes were afire.

"We need to stop," she said between breaths, "or I am going to have to turn the faucet all the way to the cold setting."

"Give me one good reason," he demanded.

"Lucas is here," she answered, voice husky. "but it all starts as a kiss and the next thing you know, it's night-light eyes and fang boners. We'd never hear the end of it."

He smiled at her and cocked his head. "Fang boners?"

Deziree laughed. "You like that, huh?" She stood up on her toes and placed her lips on his. "Come on. As much as I don't want to leave this shower right now, I'm turning into a prune and I still need to get washed up."

"Fine, but later, you're mine." He kissed her again, testing her willpower one last time before he handed her the wash cloth.

❦

While they were getting dressed, Deziree glanced at Vegas and smiled, remembering his brother was in the other room the entire time they were having their naked wrestling match in the shower. "So the vampire out there with super hearing totally knows what we were doing, doesn't he?"

Vegas opened his mouth to reply when from the living room they heard, "Yes, I heard every moan, groan, and whimper. And Dez?"

"Yes, Lucas?"

"You were pretty loud too," he replied.

Dez rolled her eyes as she pulled up her pants. "We didn't even have sex," she whispered. "He's not going to be allowed to be within miles of us when we do."

"I'm going to throttle him," Vegas said, buckling his belt and shaking his head, the smile never leaving his face. He yanked a black t-shirt down over his head. The shirt was tight, clinging to and accentuating every muscle in his torso. *God, he's gorgeous*, she thought, staring slack jawed at him.

He leaned in close to her ear, wrapping his strong arms around her and whispered, "For the record, I don't really give a shit who hears us." He turned his head and kissed her cheek before letting her go so she could finish dressing herself. Her cheeks flushed and she couldn't think of a good reason to continue putting her clothes on.

Taking a deep breath to calm her nerves, she said, "So what now? We can't just sit here. I'm going to end up going bat-shit crazy."

"I've been thinking about it," he replied, "and I think we should start at Natalia's place."

"Why?" She looked at him incredulously. "You've already been through it and the coven has already been all over it. We have no idea who is responsible for calling up the pureblood, but I'm guessing if there was any evidence of their involvement, it's long gone by now."

Vegas sat down on the corner of the bed and rubbed his hands over his head. "I know, and I agree. But there's always a chance I missed something. Plus, we've got a fresh pair of eyes with you around. I want to try one more time. I think it'd be best that we keep our movements to ourselves until we have a better picture of who might be in on it."

"Alright," she conceded, "let's do it."

CHAPTER THIRTEEN

Deziree

Deziree stepped over the threshold of the deceased records keeper's apartment, and instantly her breath was taken away. The woman had a gorgeous home. Deziree couldn't help but think it was too bad the plush living space was tainted by the girl's demise. What would ordinarily be a warm sitting room painted by sunlight now seemed cold, gray, and lifeless.

As she walked past the large couch, Deziree ran her hand over its brown suede. She could easily imagine curling up on it for hours and reading a good book, allowing herself to sink into the warm embrace of the cushions. Deziree imagined Natalia had probably done exactly that, working into the early hours of dawn as she absorbed all the information that had been handed down to her.

Throughout the apartment were knickknack shelves, each containing various baubles, bottles, and small, carved wooden boxes. The bottles each held a supply of different herbs with labels bearing the name of each inscribed in tiny gold letters. Caraway, angelica root, Spanish moss, mandrake root, and ginger were a few Dez noticed right away.

"Damiana?" she whispered to herself. Damiana was usually found in the cabinet of a witch who would sell seduction spells. Although it wasn't against coven law, it was certainly frowned upon. Anything with the power to tamper with free will was taboo.

"It's not what you think." Lucas's voice startled her as he stepped up alongside her. "Natalia wasn't like that."

"What was it for then?" She didn't mean to sound so judgmental, but there it was.

"She got it shortly after we started sleeping together." As soon as he started to reply, a smile laced with sadness lightly crept across his face, and his eyes stared off as he half lost himself in memory. He was quiet for a moment and then he turned to Deziree and the focus returned to his eyes. "Sex is absolutely incredible on damiana. Not that we needed it, but we occasionally would smoke it blended with tobacco right before we—"

"Okay," Dez interrupted, eyes shut and shaking her head, "stop. Please, just stop before I end up with a head full of images I'm unable to scrub out."

"You asked," he said with a sly smile.

"You could have just said she used it for recreational purposes."

She turned the brass knob unlocking the window and stepped out onto the balcony for some fresh air. Lucas followed. Black metal baskets hung from all three sides of the small terrace, each one overflowing with thick green leaves and blossoms. The flowers had vivid burgundy petals fading into a white center and gave off a light scent, pleasant, not too strong.

"It's beautiful here, isn't it?" he said, taking in a lung full of cool air. "She loved flowers." He took a blossom in his fingers. "Stargazer lilies were her favorite but growing

73

them would have taken too much time and effort. She chose the Madagascar periwinkle because it basically takes care of itself." He stared off into the distance. He huffed. "Being here is even harder than I thought it would be. It still doesn't feel like it's real, you know? I keep expecting her to come strolling out of her bedroom, holding a pen with her teeth, throwing her hair up into a ponytail, getting ready to sit down and dive into one tome or another for the day." He clenched his jaw and subtly shook his head. His eyes glistened with unshed tears. "We need to figure out a way to stop all of this. I wouldn't wish this feeling upon my worst enemy."

Dez did her best to force down the lump forming in her throat, grasping for some words that would help ease her friend's pain. She knew deep down that nothing she said or did was going to make him feel any better. Instead of words, she looped her arms around his and leaned her head on his shoulder. He placed a kiss on the top of her head and released a deep sigh.

"Thanks, Dez," he said, his voice quivering. He cleared his throat and continued, "We should see if Michael has dug anything up." She released his arm and the two turned and stepped back inside the apartment. Deziree walked to the library doors and peered inside. Vegas was crouched down looking through the pile of books strewn all over the floor.

"Wow," Dez muttered. "I assumed they would have collected these by now."

"That's part of the reason I wanted to get over here as soon as possible," Vegas explained. "If they take it all away, there's no way to know what's missing. I'm willing to bet the demon might have left a clue to his whereabouts."

Deziree studied the room, stopping next to the visitor chair in front of Natalia's large, wooden desk. Black and gray ash stains riddled the chair and the two square feet of carpet before it, indicating where Natalia's body had been. Deziree knelt down. There was ash, lots of it, but neither the floor nor the chair had been burned. Deziree touched the ashen spot on the floor. The moment her fingers made contact, her back arched and her skin burned. She felt as though her body were being continually rocked by invisible tendrils of electricity whipping through every cell of her body in a wild frenzy

She could hear Vegas shouting her name but he sounded so far away, as though he were yelling to her through a long, stone tunnel. Her vision went completely black and she could no longer see the room around her. Suddenly, she was assaulted with a barrage of pictures and flashes of images, each slamming into her with another jolt of pain.

Then the pain fell away, the sounds of her own screams growing distant. The air around her suddenly felt wrong. It was thick and suffocating. Shapes began to form out of the blackness surrounding her, and her vision swam as she tried to focus. A hallway came into view, the hallway outside of Natalia's apartment. *How the hell did I get out here?* she thought. She tried to call out to Vegas first, then Lucas, but no sound came out. No matter how hard she tried to stop herself, she just kept moving forward. That's when she realized she wasn't the one running the show.

Thoughts that weren't her own flitted through her mind. Vicious thoughts laced with horrific images. Someone or something screaming out in a type of agony she'd never heard before as they collapsed in a burning heap. No one told her it was hellfire. She just knew. Call it instinct, call it second nature. Whatever it was, it felt like knowledge ingrained in her from birth.

She watched helplessly as she stopped in front of Natalia's door, and a man's hand reached up in front of her and knocked. She half expected to see Lucas or Vegas answer the door. Instead, the door swung open and Natalia's face appeared, instantly shifting from a pleasant greeting to utterly terrified as she stumbled backward into her apartment. Dez felt an unexpected rush of pleasure the moment Natalia's eyes filled with fear and recognition.

Oh I really don't want to watch this, she thought as realized what she was seeing. She had no idea how it happened, but she was watching Natalia's final moments through the eyes of her killer. Her heart plummeted. An overwhelming rush of anticipation flooded her thoughts. The thrill of the hunt. He didn't need her for anything, not really. He just wanted to play with her a bit. Dez tried to close her eyes, to somehow not see the scene playing out before her, but it was no use.

The man picked Natalia up from the floor and shoved her over the desk, maliciously using her unconscious body. Her legs were twisted at awkward angles. He held her arms behind her back, arresting her movement with his hands so she couldn't move. He backhanded her with a tight fist when she began to regain consciousness, unrelenting in his abuse of her body until he'd quenched his demonic lust. Deziree felt the burning, intense arousal after each violent action.

He checked to see if the girl was still alive and then bound her to a chair before turning his attention to the library shelves. She could feel his frustration building with every book that yielded no results. Demanding information from the girl was answered with utter defiance as she spat 'Fuck you!' at him. He hit her again for her insolence, then returned to his search. Satisfaction washed over Dez when he finally found what he was looking for.

Deziree watched from the demon's eyes as he picked up and opened another ancient-looking book. The brown leather cover was so worn, the gold-embossed letters nearly flat and colorless with use, she couldn't make out the title.

Tucked between brittle pages, toward the back, was a list. The unassuming little piece of yellowed notebook paper held the names of the Guardians and each of their locations.

Deziree watched as he took the list and examined it, then felt a wicked smile creeping across his face. She heard Natalia choke back a quiet sob and Deziree looked on as he turned back to her. Blind and broken, Natalia was his to do with as he pleased. Deziree could feel the anticipation and, again, wanting in the pureblood's thoughts. He toyed with her, putting a droplet of his own blood on each of her eyelids. Deziree couldn't believe what she was seeing. The blood had done something to her, making the poor girl's battered face return to normal as if the damage was running in reverse. She had been beautiful, Deziree thought. Not in a way that required cosmetics, but a purely natural beauty. Deziree could see why Lucas had fallen so hard for this girl, and her heart broke for him.

If she had mistaken his repair of Natalia's broken face as an act of kindness on the demon's behalf, it was quickly rectified in the next image she saw. She watched in mute horror as Natalia's body started to writhe in agony and then, in a flash, burst into flames.

The images finally ceased and as her own vision returned to her, the echoes of Natalia's terrified screams and the demon's maniacal laughter boomed in her head. She slumped and she fell over. She expected to hit the floor, but Vegas's warm hands caught her instead.

"Dez!" he exclaimed, worry saturating his tone. "Hey! Dez! Are you alright?"

She coughed, her throat hot and dry as though she'd be breathing arid desert air for days.

Vegas barked a demand for water, never taking his eyes off her. "Are you okay?"

She nodded, not entirely convinced she was telling him

the truth. She was still coughing and struggling to catch her breath when Lucas returned with a bottle of water. Deziree opened the bottle and took several long gulps, cooling her throat. She closed her eyes, desperately wishing she could unsee it. All of it. She inhaled and exhaled slowly to calm the spasms racking her lungs. When she thought she'd regained most of her control, she opened her eyes to see Vegas crouched in front of her. She opened her mouth to speak and instantly regretted it. The smell of sulfur overwhelmed her senses, and bile rose in her throat. She jumped to her feet, running for the window. As her gag reflex caused her throat to constrict, she realized she wasn't going to make it. She grabbed the little black metal trash can next to Natalia's desk and emptied the contents of her stomach. As the heaves came to a stop, Dez threw the window open, desperately gasping for fresh air. She breathed long and hard to clear her lungs. Just as quickly as the sulfur smell appeared, it was gone.

"Dez, what the hell just happened?" She stared out the window as glimpses of what she had just seen flashed through her mind. Her brow furrowed as the memory of the pain and torture the demon had inflicted lingered in her mind.

Finally, she met Vegas's eyes. "I saw the whole thing."

"Tell me what you saw," Lucas said with urgency.

Deziree turned sad eyes to both vampires. "I saw everything. It ... *hurt* her but she never broke." Her stomach turned again as she paraphrased. "She wasn't awake for the worst of what he did. Despite the horrible way she died, it was over quick." Lucas frowned, his brow bending over his eyes as they clouded with tears and anger. He didn't pry for further details. "I'm so sorry," she whispered.

A tear rolled down Lucas's cheek.

"Wait. You said you *saw* everything. What does that mean?"

"Is *I don't know* an acceptable response? Because that's all I've got. Nothing like that has ever happened to me before. Something *happened* when I touched the ashes. One minute I was me and the next minute, I was him. The demon. It was like I was inside his head. I saw everything he saw. But I didn't just see what he saw. I felt his emotions. Anger. Hatred." She glanced at Lucas, who had moved to a window to stare at the Grand Canal. She dropped her voice to a whisper. "Pleasure. It was sickening. I couldn't exactly hear his thoughts, but I felt them as if they were my own."

"Like a psychic link."

"I think it was memories, his memories, of that night. It was like I *was* him."

"Did you happen to catch anything about which gateway he's going to try to open?"

"No," Deziree responded, "it wasn't exactly like I could ask. He was looking for the Guardians, I know that. I saw the list, and I know where they were."

"That could be helpful," Lucas added. He had apparently collected himself enough to rejoin the conversation.

"What do you mean?"

"If you did it here, we could go where the Guardians were murdered, and you can do your witchy-demon woo woo there too. His focus would have shifted to finding the stone and opening the gateway. Maybe we can find out his plans through these memories."

"Provided it works again," Vegas added, not sounding too confident. Dez couldn't blame him. It may have been a fluke. She'd never heard of a witch gleaning memories from ashes before, but there had also never been a witch like her before. "Do you think you can handle going through this again?"

"Yeah. It didn't kill me, so it's worth going there to see if I can do it again."

"What made you so sick?" Lucas asked.

"Sulphur. Some vampires you are." Her lungs spasmed again without warning, launching her into another coughing fit. She caught her breath enough to guzzle down the rest of the bottle of water. When she could breathe again, she added, "You're both blessed with supernatural senses and you somehow missed the smell of rotten eggs."

The two vampires exchanged confused glances, then eyed her curiously.

"What?"

"We didn't smell anything," Vegas replied.

"Really?"

"Maybe the smell was part of the memory," Lucas suggested.

"I guess," Dez replied, thought for a moment, then added, "I could do without the scratch and sniff portion of the evening."

"Now that we know this is possible, we should move," Vegas said, all business. "Where were the Guardians hiding out?"

"St. Tropez, London, Rome, Savannah, and New York."

"That makes things tougher. I thought the Guardians were all together. I know they were at one point."

"Apparently they split up," Dez said with a shrug. "It makes sense. That would be a good way to keep the stone hidden."

"It would make it really easy on us if you remembered the addresses," Lucas said, running his fingers through his hair.

"Are you kidding? I couldn't forget what I saw if I tried. I remember every detail with perfect clarity. The problem is knowing which one to go to first." Five locations meant they ran a serious risk of choosing the wrong one and not finding the demon in time. If it reached the gateway before they found the right location, none of this would matter.

"Is there anything else you think we need to know?" Vegas asked.

"No," she responded with certainty. "He didn't go after anything else here. Once he found the list, he finished up with Natalia, then left. I'm sure he didn't even spare a backward glance." He nodded but didn't say anything. She could practically hear the gears turning in his head. "How are we going to do this? We can't be in five places at once."

"You're right, we can't. It'll take some creative logistics, but I've got an idea. Are you alright to move?"

"Yeah, I'm good now."

"I'm going to make a call. We can't do this alone," Vegas said, pulling out his phone. Then he turned to Lucas. "I'm really sorry to rush you, but we're kind of on a clock here. Are you ready to leave or would you like another minute?"

Lucas was standing behind Natalia's desk fidgeting with a shiny object in his hand. He held up the object for the two of them to see and they realized it was a silver ring.

"I bought this for her from one of those little street vendors." He was staring at the ring with a far-off look in his eyes. "I bought the wrong size and it was too big so she wore it on her thumb. She only ever took it off when she was cataloging. She'd set it right here next to her laptop. This design is said to protect the wearer. Maybe if she'd been wearing the ring ..." His voice faded. He sighed and slid it onto his left ring finger. The hand balled into a tight fist.

"Let's go. She's not here anymore, and I've got a demon to *thank in person* for that."

CHAPTER FOURTEEN

Michael

Michael and Deziree stood on the *Ponte delgi Scalzi* looking out over the Grand Canal. The sound of the water flowing below was peaceful. Boats traveled the canal in their usual fashion, gliding through the water, which glowed amber in the lamplight. If it weren't for the reason behind their visit to the bridge, it could have been a romantic moment for them. He took Deziree's hand, entwining his fingers with hers. "When this is all over, we'll definitely have to take our vacation."

She nodded. "I'll be holding you to that." They shared a lingering kiss. So often, lately, someone would pull them away from each other. This time it was Kade, clearing his throat to break into their interlude.

"Sorry to interrupt you two lovebirds," Kade said with a wry smile.

"Hey, thanks for coming," Michael said, reaching a hand out and pulling his old friend into a brief hug.

"Never a problem, you know that," Kade replied, stepping back. "Deziree." He leaned in and gave her a quick kiss on the cheek. "You know, we don't need to travel all the way to Italy for the three of us to catch up. I do live right on the other side of Manhattan."

"I know," Michael responded apologetically. "Lately, we haven't gotten together nearly as often as I'd like. When this is all over, you'll have to come by Onyx for a drink with us."

"Yes," Dez added with a smile. "Maybe we will shut the place down for a night and throw a big private party." With a wink, she added, "I know the owner, so I bet I could make it happen."

"Okay," Kade said with a grin, "it's a plan then. In the meantime, what can I help you with? When you called and asked to meet alone, I was under the assumption that meant something was wrong."

Michael peered around to make sure they were safe to speak where they were. When he was sure the coast was clear, he looked at Kade and asked, "You trust your people, right?"

"Of course, with my life," Kade responded simply. "Why do you ask?"

"We need a favor and it is going to require some manpower," Dez replied. "We need to know we can trust everyone involved."

"What's this about?" Kade leaned back on the bridge, relaxing his weight against the stone.

"The demon attack," Michael explained. "We have reason to believe that someone inside the covens summoned that demon. It's the only possible way the damned thing could have made it onto this plane. We have a few leads we need to go investigate. That's where you come in. If we give you a few addresses, can you place men there to guard the properties until we arrive?"

"Absolutely," Kade replied without hesitation. "Where am I sending them?"

"One address is right in New York," Dez explained as

she handed him a piece of paper with the addresses written on it. "It's a fifth floor walk-up in the West Village. The second address is in Savannah, Georgia, in the Victorian district."

"When do you need them there?" Kade asked.

"As soon as possible," Michael said. "The faster we can secure those locations, the better. We can't chance anyone getting in there and getting rid of anything."

"Okay," Kade said. "I will make some calls and get my guys to head to both places immediately. Can I ask what these addresses have to do with the demon?"

"It's where two of the five Guardians were killed," Dez replied.

"We are leaving tonight for Rome," Michael said, "then St. Tropez. From St. Tropez, we are going to London. After London, we will be on our way to the States, but depending on how long the three European stops take, it is going to be a few days before we arrive."

"When do you two take off?" Kade asked.

"It's three of us actually," Michael said. "Lucas is with us." Michael glanced at his watch. "Our flight leaves in about three hours. He should be leaving for the airport with our bags right about now, so unfortunately, we have to go pretty soon if we want to make our flight."

"Why wasn't Lucas at the council meeting?"

"The dead records keeper was his girlfriend," Dez explained. "We aren't sure who knows they were together, or that he was actually the first one to find her body. We have kept his presence as quiet as possible to avoid tipping anyone off that we might know more than we are letting on."

"Understood," Kade replied. "You go catch your flight and I will place my calls to get my people moving. You'll keep in touch?"

"We will," Michael replied, reaching out to shake the

vampire's hand again. "Kade, thank you. We will keep you in the loop on what we find. And please, don't let anyone here in Venice know what you're up to."

"Not a problem at all, old friend. Be safe, alright?"

"We will and you do the same."

Michael took Deziree's hand and the two of them headed in the direction of the private limousine waiting for them. When they were on the way to the airport, they discussed what they should do next. One thing they agreed on was to call Cassandra. They wouldn't tell her the entire story, but it was best if she at least knew they were looking into a few things. Inaction would be far more suspicious than a little white lie.

CHAPTER FIFTEEN

Dez

"Hey, Cass," Dez greeted when her adoptive mother answered the call.

"Why do you insist on calling me by that name, Deziree?" she scolded, her voice remaining perfectly calm. "It sounds like the name of a pet dog or a cow." Deziree laughed and shook her head. "Anyway, how are you?"

"I'm good," Dez responded. "Exhausted, and I could really go for a massage right now, but I'm good otherwise. How are things on your end?"

"You know the covens," Cassandra said flippantly. "They wouldn't be happy if there wasn't some sort of dramatic situation afoot. Not that I am downplaying the severity of this situation, but really, it sounds like a hen house in here right now."

Deziree laughed. For the majority of the time, Cassandra was prim and proper, the very picture of a professional. But there were moments when she slipped into something more sarcastic. The combination of her centuries of wisdom and lack of patience for anything she deemed to be a waste of time occasionally manifested in snarky comments about whatever happened to be pissing her off in the moment.

"I wanted to give you a call and let you know we are leaving town for a little while."

"Oh really?" Dez could picture Cassandra sitting in her office, phone to her ear and eyebrows furrowed.

"Yeah, we will be back though. We are going to take a trip to do some sniffing around. It's better than just sitting here doing nothing." Deziree felt bad lying to her; she believed omission was the same as telling someone a complete lie. However, she and Vegas had discussed it and it was important to maintain a level of stealth. They didn't want to alarm anyone, especially Cassandra.

"Alright, darling," Cassandra replied. "At this point, I wish I could go with you. An escape from all this would be bliss right about now. Alas, my place is here. I know you can handle yourself and you have a strong ally in Michael, but I hope you will still call and let me know you're alright, for the sake of my peace of mind."

"Of course I will. Talk to you soon."

"Goodbye, dear."

With that, Dez hung up the phone as they pulled into the airport entrance.

CHAPTER SIXTEEN

Michael

They found Lucas waiting for them, luggage already checked. He had a caddy of paper coffee cups and handed one to Dez.

"It's coffee mixed with tempero," Lucas said as he handed a cup to Michael. "It's not going to taste pleasant, but with all the traveling we are going to be doing in the next few days, better safe than sorry," said Lucas. "I stashed some in my checked luggage before we left the manor. I added extra cream to the coffee to cool it down so you should be able to drink it right away."

"How are you doing? Are you holding up okay?" Michael asked.

"I never thought I'd say this," Lucas replied, "but I'm ready to get the hell out of Venice. I used to love this city but now it's just one gross bitter memory."

"You have *some* good memories here," Dez added.

"You're right. But every good one ends with me finding the dead body of the only woman I ever loved."

"Just try to hold on to the good times," she said, placing a comforting hand on his shoulder. He nodded then took a deep breath as he checked his watch. "We'd better get going." They all took big gulps until their cups were empty then tossed them in the garbage on the way to the gate.

As they walked the length of the concourse, Michael could see the exhaustion starting to take its toll on Deziree. As soon as he saw it on her face, he felt it himself. The short flight would give them all a chance to kick back and recharge.

CHAPTER SEVENTEEN

They touched down in Rome and a quick cab ride took them from the airport to the Colosseum. They paid the cab driver handsomely to wait for them. He pulled into a nearby parking space and shut off the engine. Lucas remained in the car to be sure the cab driver didn't just drive away with the large sum of money and their luggage. A short walk brought them to the Guardian's address. The large, stone edifice contained many small apartments, and when they arrived at their destination, they were not surprised to find it locked. With no effort at all, Vegas twisted the doorknob until the locking mechanism inside the door shattered under the pressure of his grip.

"Show off," Dez teased.

The apartment was simple, decorated in a minimalist style. Each room had the barest of furnishings and no artwork adorned the walls. The domicile had two bedrooms, one of which had been set up as an office. A small wooden desk sat by the window and there were bookcases against each wall. It appeared the only luxury the Guardian had indulged in were the myriad of books lining each shelf. Deziree read off some of the titles, all of which were classic works ranging from *To Kill a Mockingbird* to *The Divine Comedy*.

"I don't see an ash mark anywhere," Vegas said, panning around the room. "It's not like there is much to hide it under. I wonder if they've already had someone in here to clean up. I'm going to go look around the bedroom." He stepped out of the room and Deziree continued looking at the books.

"Dez!" Vegas called out. She followed his voice into the bedroom. "Found it." He pulled the blankets back to reveal a black shadow of ash lying on top of the sheets.

"I will never understand the science behind hellfire and how a person can burn to death and not scorch anything else."

"Hellfire isn't scientific. It's mystical," he explained. "Hellfire isn't about burning material. It's a violent magic that incinerates the person's soul. The body burning is just a side effect."

Dez was lost in thought staring at the blackened sheets. Not too long ago that had been a person. Not human, but a person nonetheless. And now they're just gone. She looked down at her own hands, and for a split second, she allowed herself to wonder if she would one day turn into one of these things. A creature that could be capable of incinerating another being without remorse. She squeezed her eyes shut and pushed the thought away.

"Are you sure you're ready to do this?"

Though she knew what was coming, she nodded anyway. She shook her hands in the air in an effort to prepare her nerves for the assault they were about to receive. She shut her eyes and rolled her neck around, releasing as much of the tension as possible before she touched anything.

"I'll be right here," Vegas assured her. Their eyes met and she forced a smile.

She kneeled and slowly reached out to touch the ash. The familiar shock ran through her body and again, pain shot through her head as the images came to her in a savage barrage.

The demon walked to the door quietly. This time he didn't knock. Instead he wiggled the door handle to find it was locked. A wave of his long fingers, a clicking sound from the lock, and he let himself into the apartment. He silently stepped over the threshold and closed his eyes, reaching out with his senses. He was hoping to feel something but it wasn't there. The concern for stealth left him. The moment the demon stepped into the bedroom, the sleeping Guardian burst into flames.

Deziree's vision returned to her quickly. The results were the same as before. Vegas was waiting with a large mixing bowl and a glass of water.

Deziree drank the water down and took a few deep breaths. She anticipated the sulfurous smell and when it didn't come immediately, she thought she might actually catch a break. But as soon as she got to her feet, it slammed into her abruptly and she pitched over, spewing into the bowl.

She collected herself and went to the bathroom to rinse her mouth. She was glad to find a large bottle of mouthwash in one of the cabinets. After swishing out her mouth repeatedly, she rinsed out the sink and joined Vegas in the kitchen. He had washed the bowl and was drying it with a hand towel when she rounded the corner of the hallway. He returned the bowl and towel back to where he'd found them.

"You cleaned up in there, right? We've got to leave the least amount of evidence possible."

"I did but I used about half of the bottle of mouthwash first. That's going to get old really fast."

"What did you see?"

"It was nothing like Natalia. He broke in, in the middle

of the night. The Guardian was sleeping. He stepped into the apartment, tried to feel for something, and when he got no results, he walked in and burned him. There was no ceremony to it this time. I don't think the Guardian ever even knew he was here. He was trying to sense the Sentinel Stone. When he didn't find anything, there was no hesitation. He torched the Guardian and turned his back on the place. He didn't bother even searching the apartment for it. In a matter of seconds, he knew the stone wasn't here."

"That's good! This may all go a lot faster than we had anticipated. If the demon knows whether or not the stone is present, that means he only killed this Guardian to prevent him or her from notifying the others. We will know in a matter of minutes at each residence whether or not there's any info we can use."

A very good point, she thought. "Okay, let's go then." She started toward the door. "We still have a lot of work to do and this thing is moving a lot faster than we had anticipated."

"Are you good to keep going? When you went through this at Natalia's, it kicked your ass."

"I'll be fine," she replied. "It wasn't as bad this time. There was very little emotion and it didn't feel nearly as intense. More than anything, he was just in a hurry, so we should be too."

With the exception of the broken lock, they left the apartment just as they'd found it, and as soon as they were in the hall, Vegas pulled out his cell phone to make a call.

"Lucas, get the three of us on to the next flight to St. Tropez."

CHAPTER EIGHTEEN

Dez

"Vegas!" Deziree called out. "I think I found where I want to go on our next vacation!"

She was standing in the middle of the enormous living room of the equally enormous house. Everything about the estate was the polar opposite of the last Guardian's home. This house looked lived in. There were magazines stacked neatly on the coffee table. A fifty-two inch flat-screen television took up a good portion of one wall, with bookcases below it filled with DVDs. When they came in the door, they passed a coat room filled with evidence of the living: sun chairs, tote bags, scuba gear, and several sun umbrellas.

"I'd be afraid to get the place dirty," Vegas commented. Everything about the house was white—the exterior walls, interior walls, the furniture, the floors. "This Guardian must have made a killing living in the human world."

"This one was definitely female," Dez stated matter of factly. "Check out all the pictures."

All over the living room and hallway walls were framed pictures. They all had one woman in common, blonde and smiling in each. She was a pretty woman with a petite frame. Judging by the pictures, the little Guardian liked to party.

"Boy, she sure likes to drink, doesn't she? Out by the pool, on the beach, on a boat. She's like the Sam I Am of liquor. Almost all of the pictures feature her with a fruity-looking beverage and I bet those drinks aren't virgin. I had no idea angels drank alcohol." Deziree approached the sliding glass doors which spanned the width of the entire room. "Wow," she said in awe. From the living room, the view was breathtaking. Palm trees waved in the breeze, over a long sloping hill and then the ocean stretched out as far as the eyes could see. "I could totally get used to this place." An awful part of her quietly wondered how much a place like this ran for, and how quickly it would be on the market.

"With all the blinding white," Vegas began, "it should be fairly easy to find where she was burned."

"Yes, it should," Dez agreed.

The two went in search of the ash spot checking each room. Vegas stopped in the kitchen and grabbed two bottles of water. Dez cocked an eyebrow at him. "Is this really the time to stop for snacks?"

"A certain half-demon I know is going to get very thirsty when we find what we're looking for." She rolled her eyes at him.

They walked through the entire house with no luck.

"It has to be here somewhere." Vegas checked each of the five bedrooms one more time while Dez peered out the window at the double pool and hot tub on the back side of the house.

"Vegas," Dez said, "we have more house to check out." She gestured for him to look out the window and pointed at the pool house and gazebo on the far side of the pool.

They took the sliding glass door to the patio. The sun

reflecting off the white concrete nearly blinded both of them. They walked around the perimeter of the pool, briefly stopping at the gazebo only to discover there were no ash marks present. They continued on to the pool house. Finding the door unlocked, they let themselves in and saw it was decorated the same as the main house. The lavish guest house had two bedrooms, a theater room, a shower, and a large wine cellar.

"See?" Dez started. "She was a total booze hound."

"An alcoholic with very good and very expensive taste in vineyards," Vegas added as he inspected the labels of a few of the vintages. "Let's check the bedrooms first and then work our way back to the front door."

They split up, each taking a bedroom, and each coming up empty handed. When they came back out into the hallway, they each shook their heads and returned to the theater room. Vegas looked for a light switch as the theater was the only room on the property not painted bright white. He found them behind a long black curtain and flipped all of them on.

She stood in front of the twenty chaise lounges which served for seating. "Bingo! We have ash." She pointed to the seat in front of her at exactly center row.

"Perfect," Vegas stated. "You ready?"

"Yup." Deziree knelt down by the chair and touched the ash, this time fully prepared for the impact the process would have on her body.

Much like the last Guardian's home, the demon had let himself in and taken almost the same journey they had to get here. First through the main house, then he made his way to the smaller house. He performed the same search in both houses, trying to feel for the stone's magic and when he couldn't sense it, he went on a mission looking for the Guardian. He found her in the theater room alone watching an action movie. The volume was loud enough she never even heard him coming. Deziree watched as the Guardian began to burn and the demon turned his back on the scene. The violence of gunfire and explosions playing out on the screen behind him provided a sound-track for the angel's horrific death as the demon left the room.

When her vision returned, Vegas had her bottle of water waiting. She drank down the entire bottle and then stood up and headed for the shower room. When the sulfur smell hit her, it wasn't as strong as she had smelled at the previous times and she was able to make it through without getting sick to her stomach.

"Either it wasn't as strong this time," she said as she breathed through the nausea, "or I am getting used to it, which is unsettling all on its own. Yay for progress." She didn't particularly like the idea of getting used to anything having to do with demons. It may be in her blood, but she had no desire to become a monster, and that was exactly what they were dealing with.

"Did you see anything new?"

"Nope," she answered, "same shit, different city."

"Alright," Vegas replied. "London?"

"London it is."

CHAPTER NINETEEN

Michael

The car ride back to the airport passed quickly. Deziree had slipped into a deep sleep, curled into the crook of Michael's arm almost as soon as they were back in the car. Michael told Lucas what happened in the St. Tropez house and expressed his concern about the turn of events.

"She made a comment," he whispered, rubbing his hand lightly up and down her arm, "about getting used to the effects of doing whatever it is that she's doing when she touches the ashes."

"Do you think there's more to it?"

"I don't know," he replied, shaking his head. "The fact that she's even making these connections is a little worrisome. That demon being here on our plane might be enhancing her demon side. I can't wait for all of this to be over so we can focus on her. I don't want her to lose her humanity." He was silent for a few beats and then he turned to Lucas, meeting his brother's eyes.

"Her aura still reads well. She still has humanity left in there but I *will* say her aura has become a little bit darker in the last few days. But it's nowhere close to black like a pureblood's. Just keep an eye on her and we'll see how things develop."

Michael couldn't hide his concern. They'd always suspected that she'd manifest some sort of demon abilities, but it never occurred to them that another demon is what would trigger it. Lucas put a hand on his shoulder. "I'm sure she'll be fine. She's tough as nails. Try not to worry."

CHAPTER TWENTY

Michael

London held more of the same. The Guardian who lived in the Hyde Park flat was murdered in the same fashion as all the others. His ashes were found on the bathroom floor as though he were attacked while climbing out of the shower.

As they made their way back down to the car, Dez's voice was raspy. "I think we should hit Savannah first. I'm exhausted beyond reason but I want to get this done. After Savannah, we will hit the New York apartment if we still need to. I really want to sleep in my own bed for just one night. I am so tired I can't even think straight. We can get settled at my place and regroup there."

Worry worked its way further into Michael's thoughts. She sounded so worn out and her usual good-natured sarcasm seemed to be lost under all the fatigue. He wanted so badly to believe it was due to the non-stop travel they'd put themselves through in the last few days, but he wasn't convinced.

"We can do that," he replied. "We'll fly first class to Savannah so you can be more comfortable."

"Good idea," Deziree said. He caught the sight of dark circles forming under her eyes. Upon closer inspection, he could plainly see that something wasn't right. He tried to figure it out but couldn't pinpoint the change.

"Hey, Dez," he said, grasping her hand and gently pulling her to a stop. "Are you feeling okay? Aside from being tired, I mean."

"Why do you ask?" Her words were devoid of their usual warmth.

"Something seems off with you," he explained. "I can't wrap my head around what it is but something isn't right."

"Why should you be trying to wrap your head around anything other than our mission?" she sneered, words dripping with venom. "Maybe it has something to do with how gross I feel. Between the fact that I haven't showered in a few days and all this demon shit, I feel nasty. You have no idea what it's like to be in his head. He's all hatred and cold detachment, totally unfeeling and ruthless to no end. I want all of this to be done and over with." She paused and her eyes glazed over as she stared off at nothing. "More than anything, I just want this to be over."

"We will figure this out, Dez," Michael replied, putting a finger under her chin to force her to make eye contact with him. "Everything will work out. I promise." He tried to sound reassuring, but he found it hard to pour conviction into his words when even he wasn't convinced. "Maybe it's time we brought Cassandra in to let her know what's been going on."

"No," she snapped. "You said it yourself, Michael. The less people involved at this point, the better." She yanked her head away from his hand and he was taken aback by her sudden use of his given name. It had been *years* since she'd called him by his name in a serious manner and never with such malice. The sound of it being spat at him stung. "I don't need to be protected and I don't need to be showered with pity. I need a hot shower and a nap."

She turned and stormed off toward the waiting taxi, leaving Michael stunned. He shook his head and followed her to the car. After she climbed in, he stood outside the car and glanced back at the building. He was overcome by a foreboding feeling. He hoped, in the deepest part of his heart, that her acidity had been caused by the events of the past week and not by something more permanent.

CHAPTER TWENTY-ONE

Michael

They arrived at Heathrow airport, booked their tickets, and had a couple of hours to pass while they waited for boarding. Michael was relieved to learn Lucas was able to get all three of them first-class seats for their flight. He pulled his phone out of his pocket and dialed Kade's number. It rang twice and after greetings were exchanged, Kade asked if they had arrived in the States yet.

"Not yet," Michael replied. "We're flying into DC, and then to Savannah. We should be there in about fourteen hours or so. Have your people reported any visitors at either place yet?"

"No, nothing yet," Kade replied, "it's been perfectly quiet. Were you really expecting someone to show?"

"No, not really. I just figured I would check. When I get to Savannah, I'll let you know so you can give them the all clear."

"You sure you don't need them for anything?" Kade asked. "I can have them wait if you'd like."

"Thanks, but I don't think we'll need them. Everything has been quiet up until now and my guess is the only people who would need to go to either property already have what they were looking for."

"Better to be safe than sorry. For my own peace of mind, I'll keep them at a short distance."

"Thank you for your help," he said, not wanting to insult the vampire by refusing his offer, but the extra muscle was really not needed. The three of them could easily take care of themselves.

"Anytime," Kade replied, a smile in his voice.

"It's likely we will need you in New York. When we get back, we'll meet at the West Village address."

"Sounds like a plan. Call me then."

"I will. Thank you again." Michael hung up his phone, confident Kade could be counted on as an ally.

Michael's mind churned with what the near future held. The demon and the stone were both in the wind as far as they could tell. If they did manage to catch up with the thing, they still needed to figure out a way to stop him from opening the gateway. Killing a pureblood demon wasn't exactly an easy task. Then there was still the traitor in the covens to deal with. Allies were going to be necessary. Allies and evidence. Without support or witnesses to back them up, making an accusation of that magnitude could accomplish the equivalent of signing their own death warrants. Michael felt Kade was a good man and an even better vampire. He was fiercely loyal to those he represented in the Walker coven and he had their explicit trust. His people would stand behind him if they needed them, regardless of what was asked.

Michael headed toward the gate, briefly stopping by the coffee vendor to grab a cup for Lucas and Dez. When he returned to them, she was asleep against Lucas's shoulder as he played a game on his phone. Michael hoped for what seemed like the hundredth time that sleep would cure what was ailing Deziree.

CHAPTER TWENTY-TWO

Asmodeus

The demon sat bolt upright in his chair. Several times in the last few days he'd felt a tingling at the corners of his mind, as though another demon had been trying to reach out to him. But it couldn't be possible. When the witch summoned him, she had called him *by name.* Had she tried an open summoning, she could have ended up with anyone shadowing her doorstep, but she had specifically asked for him. *Did she bring forth another? But why?* He had already made all the progress he needed and was now laying low, waiting for the next full moon to pull on its power and open the gateway. Now that he had the Sentinel Stone, there was nothing left to do but wait.

He closed his eyes and reached out into the ether with his mind. It took a few minutes but he found it before long. He waited for the other to feel him there and advance but nothing happened. He edged closer with his mind and found a dull humming in response. *Ah, he's unconscious. Even better.*

He concentrated harder, pushing his will, and invaded the mind of the other presence. The unknown demon was dreaming of a drinking establishment of some sort. A sour mixture of liquor and human sweat permeated the air. He drifted above the floor in a plume of black smoke, looking down over the crowd in an attempt to discover his target lurking among them. When he wasn't able to pinpoint the other mind, he swooped down to the edge of the dance floor and materialized into the form of the human host he had taken. He surveyed each of the faces, searching their eyes for a hint betraying the demon hidden away inside. His confusion turned to anger with each human soul he found staring back at him. One last cursory glance across the sea of people finally told him whose mind he'd occupied.

Her piercing blue eyes locked onto him, filled first with fear. Then curiosity. Finally, fury. All in the span of just seconds.

He started toward her. The closer he got to her, the humans writhing on the dance floor started to fade into nothingness until it was just the two of them standing a few feet apart.

"Well," he sneered with disgust, "what do we have here?"

"I could say the same, demon." The contempt in her words was palpable. The overhead fans blew her black hair over her pale skin. She didn't appear threatened by his presence. Her body language was confident: her back straight as an arrow with her arms crossed over her chest. A few moments passed as they studied each other in silence and then a gun materialized in the girl's hand. Her thumb reached up and cocked the hammer back, her eyes never wavering from him.

"You know as well as I do, that silly thing won't do anything to me here," he said with a self-assured smile.

"And where is *here*, exactly?" she asked.

"Well now, child," he replied, "*you're* going to have to

answer that one." He raised his arms, looking around the nightclub. "This is your dream after all."

"I'm dreaming." It wasn't a question. She genuinely didn't seem to know. She paused for a moment and then continued. "So you're just a figment of my imagination? Then I should be able to just think you away."

"Not quite," he explained, clasping his hands behind his back and taking a few steps in her direction. "It is true we are in your dream, but I am a figment of nobody's imagination. I came here looking for you." He leaned in by her shoulder, took a long sniff of her scent, and stepped back. "I'm trying to figure out what you are, exactly. You don't smell like a demon. You reek of human and parasite. Humans can't enter the ether, not on their own. Neither can the parasites. What are you?"

"What am *I*? What are *you*? You're in *my* dream, dick. And what do you mean by *parasite*?"

"Oh yes. I forget the limitations of humans. The word in your world for their kind is 'vampire,' but let's call a spade a spade, shall we? They're parasites, feeding off the blood of their hosts. They're no different than ticks, really, but enough about them. What are you? And why have you been trying to get into my mind?"

She hesitated before answering, eyeing him curiously. Whatever internal argument she was having over how much information to give ended and she finally spoke.

"I'm half demon and half witch. As for getting into your mind, I don't even know how to do what you're talking about. Besides, why would I be doing that?"

"Isn't that what I just asked you, half-blood?" His patience was running thin.

"How about you answer one of my questions for a change? Who are you?"

"I have gone by many names through the ages. Asmodeus is the name I prefer." When he spoke his name, the barest flash of recognition and panic crossed her face but was quickly replaced by her previous calm facade. "I see you've heard of me."

"Not really. I do, however, think it is time for you to leave."

"I'm afraid you don't control when you wake up, half-blood, not as long as I'm here. Now, answer my question."

"I already told you, I don't know what you're talking about."

"Recently, I find myself repeating this with your kind. I do not take kindly to being lied to." He stared deep into the girl's eyes, willing the hellfire to erupt in her abdomen and consume her body.

Nothing happened.

He tried again and received the same results.

"Why won't you burn?" His anger boiled inside him.

"How should I know?" He searched her eyes and saw she was telling the truth. He opened his mouth to speak when a voice suddenly boomed through the air around them.

Hey, it's time to wake up.

They both watched as the room faded away.

She smiled triumphantly. "It's been fun but it's time for you to go, asshole."

The remainder of the room blinked out of existence and then she was gone. The demon was once again sitting in his dingy Rio de Janeiro hotel room. He got up and walked to the window. He breathed in the night air and nearly choked on the stink of humanity.

Soon. Soon, we will overrun this cesspool and claim it for our own.

CHAPTER TWENTY-THREE

Dez

"Hey, Dez. It's time to wake up." Vegas shook her shoulder gently, pulling her from sleep. "We're boarding in a minute. Once we're on the plane, you can go back to sleep."

Dez's eyes fluttered open and then she jolted awake, quickly sitting up, breathing heavily.

"Hey, it's alright," Vegas said calmly. "You're alright. We're at the airport."

"I saw the demon," she said, her hand on her chest.

"What? Where?" Vegas asked.

"I was dreaming. I was back at home, at Onyx, walking the floor like any other night. Then he just appeared out of nowhere. He had pale, gray skin, and black hair slicked back."

"That sounds like him," Lucas said.

"See? Lucas has seen him. There's no mistaking it. It was *him*." Her voice was laced with disgust. "I thought it was just a dream at first, but once I knew he was in my dream, I couldn't do anything to make him go away. I had no control. He told me as long as he was there, he controlled how long it went on."

"What did he say to you?" Vegas asked.

"He said he could feel me trying to get into his head. I'm guessing he was talking about the connection I have been making at the murder scenes, but he had no idea what I was doing. He didn't mention anything about the stone or the murders. He didn't even know who or what I was." She paused sifting through the details of the encounter. "He told me his name."

"Who is it?"

"Asmodeus."

"You have got to be kidding me!" Vegas leaned back in his chair, shaking his head in disbelief.

"I know. I did not see that coming. He didn't know who I was though. I am one hundred percent certain. He was clueless that I was even half demon until I told him so."

"This changes things," Vegas said, leaning forward on his knees. He searched Deziree's eyes for doubt. "Can you still go through with this?"

"Are you serious? I'm more than fine with it! It doesn't matter who he is, he's a threat."

"Hello?" Lucas interrupted them, clearly feeling left out of the conversation. "Who is Asmodeus?"

Vegas stared into Dez's eyes. Never turning to look at Lucas, he replied, "Asmodeus is Deziree's father."

"Your father? How do you know?"

"I could feel it. And when I realized who he was, everything else clicked. That's why I can access his thoughts. That's why he can't burn me," Deziree said, leaning back in the hard plastic concourse seating.

"That's a brave assumption. What makes you so sure?" Lucas asked.

The airline attendant announced they were boarding the first-class passengers and Deziree stood up. They grabbed their carry-on luggage, handed their tickets to the flight attendant, and headed for the jetway. Once inside, she explained.

"He tried when I didn't give him any information. At first, I didn't even know he was doing it. I didn't feel anything at all. He got pissed when it wouldn't work and flat out asked me why, like I would know."

"Maybe it was because it was a dream," Lucas postulated.

"No," Dez replied. "He was pretty sure of himself. It was a genuine surprise to him when it didn't work."

"I remember reading somewhere that it's believed demons can't burn other demons," Vegas said. "Maybe your heritage actually saved your life."

"Maybe. Either way, I don't think he knows what we're up to, but I don't think we should waste any time once we get to Savannah."

The three of them each took one of the private suites and once their things were situated, Deziree peeked up over the top of her seat. Vegas was in the suite right behind her and Lucas was in the suite to her right. She folded her arms on the back of the seat and watched the vampire, who was too busy rummaging through the complimentary snack tray to notice her.

"Hey," she said. "You should come up here for a second." She smiled like a little kid. Vegas stood and she sat up. She tugged the front of his shirt until his lips bumped her own. "I want to apologize," she said. "I was a total bitch back at Hyde Park and I'm sorry. It doesn't excuse it, but I was beyond angry and not thinking straight. It's not your fault and I shouldn't have taken it out on you." She put a hand on each side of his head and placed a kiss on his forehead, then one on his cheek, then one on his lips. She could feel him smile beneath her lips.

"Apology accepted on two conditions," he said.

She quirked an eyebrow. "There are conditions for accepting my apology?"

"Yes," he replied, "but it's for your own good. First condition is as soon as we are in the air, you order something to eat. They have a great dinner menu on this flight and you haven't eaten anything substantial in a few days."

"I can agree to that," she said. "What is the other condition?"

"As soon as you are done eating, call the attendant, ask for turn down service, and sleep through the rest of the flight. You need it and this is probably going to be your best opportunity for the next couple days."

"Your terms are reasonable," she replied with a wink, then her face furrowed and she got serious. "You really need to do the same." She raised her voice a little to be sure the other vampire heard her. "You and Lucas both."

Lucas leaned forward in his suite so he could yell into theirs "Don't drag me into your back-alley deals."

Deziree smiled. Things were far from being alright but this, the way the three of them joked together, felt good. It felt familiar. She hated things being strained between her and Vegas and having this reconciliation, no matter how small, made her feel like a huge weight had been lifted from her shoulders. She also knew he was completely right. She hadn't eaten much more than a few protein bars in the last two days and she felt weak and drained because of it. She knew the two vampires would need a little downtime too.

She kissed Vegas a few more times and when she leaned back to look in his eyes, he reached his hand up to her cheek and pulled her back to him. He kissed her with just the right balance of tenderness and urgency. It was both passionate and loving and it took her breath away. With everything that had been going on for the last few days, she needed to be with him. She needed the reminder that she was more than just a half-blooded monster.

By the time they broke the kiss, they were both actively trying to calm their nerves. "Your fangs are showing," she whispered in his ear.

"How are my eyes?"

Dez leaned back and looked in his eyes. They were emitting an unmistakable soft glow.

"Let's put it this way," she said. "I hope you brought sunglasses or there's a good chance you're going to freak out the other passengers."

An attendant passed by and he pecked her cheek, then sat down. Deziree took her seat again and relaxed against the plush headrest. She closed her eyes and immediately felt herself start to drift. Remembering the deal she made with Vegas, she opened her eyes and grabbed the menu.

CHAPTER TWENTY-FOUR

Dez

After a quick layover at Dulles International, their second plane touched down at Hilton Head International in Savannah, Georgia, and Vegas had to wake Deziree up. She had managed to sleep through most of the flight and never once received a visit from her unwanted guest. She wiped the sleep from her eyes and stood, stretching. She reached into the overhead compartment for her carry-on.

"You look rested," Vegas said behind her.

"I feel great," she replied, yanking the bag down into her seat.

"Good. Here, let me have that," Vegas said, taking the bag from her.

Deziree stepped into the walkway, catching sight of Lucas's empty suite. "Where did he get off to?"

"He went in search of coffee."

They waded through the crowds and when they got to the end of the causeway, Lucas was waiting with a caddy of coffee.

"Hey," Dez said in a cheery tone, "déjà vu."

"I ordered a car. It's by the curb," Lucas said, handing

them each a cup. "I am sick of riding in cramped taxis, so I got a limousine. They already loaded our luggage into the trunk and we are ready to go."

"What would we do without you?" Dez teased, pecking Lucas on the cheek.

"Someone's chipper!" Lucas exclaimed happily, sipping his coffee.

"I'm feeling much better," she said, sipping hers too.

They kept a brisk pace and were soon outside. Vegas pulled out his phone to place his scheduled call to Kade as soon as they'd settled into the car. Deziree gave the address to the driver and he put the car in gear, heading for their destination.

Once inside the lavish Victorian mansion, it took them longer than they'd expected to find the Guardian's remains. The twelve-bedroom house was labyrinthine. They found the ash outline in the large office library. Floor-to-ceiling mahogany shelves yielded carefully preserved first editions and many classics. The furniture was all old, elaborately carved, and kept in pristine condition.

The ash outline was spread over the man's desk and chair. A piece of crisp, white paper lay on the desk with a pen where the Guardian's hand might have rested. On the page, in fluid script were the words, *Someone is coming to get me. I can feel it.* Deziree shivered when she saw the words.

"Looks like he knew what was going to happen to him. Maybe one of his powers was foresight," Lucas said, taking a seat on the leather couch, grabbing up a newspaper but tossing it away when he discovered it was old.

"Ready?" Vegas asked, holding up the water bottle in his hand. Dez nodded.

In the vision, the demon melted the doorknob in his hand. He was much angrier than he had been in previous visions, the tedious search for the Sentinel Stone starting to grate on him. She could feel his patience wearing thin.

Asmodeus stepped gingerly through the house and entered the office where the Guardian was sitting and working. The Guardian's body turned red-hot and burned to a black, charred husk. The pen dropped to the desk. Asmodeus stopped to see what was written on the paper, then laughed maniacally.

He pulled out his phone but Deziree's sight failed too soon and she didn't catch whom he was calling. Just a screen with a bunch of blurred numbers she couldn't quite make out.

As soon as she'd returned to herself, she downed the bottle of water, gasping and choking for breath. "He made a phone call." She sputtered as some water went down the wrong pipe. "I couldn't see who he called, but he made a call."

"Damn," he said, "that would have been a nice break. All we would have needed was that number and we could easily figure out who was behind all of this."

This time she regained her composure quicker than she had before. She fought the nausea, and didn't find herself as close to throwing up as she had before.

"I wonder if I can go back in," Dez pondered aloud. Before the other two could say anything, she touched the ash again, her body readied for the assault. The memory played out as it had before, but this time it cut off before the demon even made it to the Guardian's office. "Dammit."

"What happened?" Vegas asked. They listened intently as she explained that the second trip through the memory actually yielded less information than the first.

"I think he's figured out a way to push me out," she added. Vegas dialed Kade and waited as it rang.

"There's only one more address," Lucas said. "The stone must be there."

"Or at least it *was* there," Vegas corrected. They

exchanged wary glances. Kade picked up. "We're on our way to the New York address. We believe the demon was there and got the Sentinel Stone from there. He is long gone by now, so you can call off your men. We'll be there soon."

CHAPTER TWENTY-FIVE

Michael

As requested, Kade's men had cleared out of the apartment. Kade remained behind and met them in the living room. They split up but the West Village apartment was small. Most New York apartments were. A superficial check yielded results.

"In here!" Dez called , and the men convened in the sparsely decorated room where she knelt beside the bed. A large safe had been built into the wall of the apartment, camouflaged by wallpaper which matched the walls. It was wide open so they could see the contents. It might have been a safe place to hide a precious artifact from regular humans or even casters, but few things in the world were demon-proof.

The ash outline was splayed over the carpet. Dez took a deep breath. Michael knelt beside her. He'd learned to carry water with him for each vision. He produced a glistening bottle and put a hand on her shoulder.

"One more time," he said, hoping to offer her some comfort. She nodded.

"One more time?" Kade asked.

"You'll see," Lucas replied.

Dez closed her eyes and touched the ash.

CHAPTER TWENTY-SIX

Asmodeus knew without a doubt the stone was there. He could feel the essence of the brimstone growing stronger as he neared the Guardian's apartment. This time he broke the doorknob with complete disregard for how loud he was being. There were no Guardians left to notify, so he had no worries of others being alerted.

He opened the door and caught the Guardian off guard in her sitting room. She jumped to her feet, the book she had been reading clattered to the floor. He instantly called upon the hellfire and her body crumpled to the ground writhing in excruciating pain. He released the hellfire and the Guardian panted with relief. After a few moments, she started to regain herself. She moved to get to her feet and he called upon the hellfire again. She dropped to the ground, screaming in agony. Again, he released the hellfire and crouched beside her withered body.

"I have just illustrated a very important lesson to you. I have the power to bring you to your knees, but you needn't suffer at all if you simply tell me where the stone is."

"No," she croaked between ragged breaths.

He called upon the hellfire once again, waited a few moments, and released it.

"Obviously, you are hard of hearing. Tell me where the stone is," he said, taking a fist full of her hair in his hands and yanking her to her knees.

She cried out and struggled for breath, and finally managed to sputter, "I don't know where the stone is."

"I can feel it. I know it's here. I will never understand why you pitiful, insignificant creatures insist on lying to superior beings. You all belong on your knees ... satisfying demons just like me." He knew she was lying, but knew he didn't need her to find the stone either. "I suppose you wouldn't lie to me after feeling the fires of Hell in your bowels." His lie was just as apparent as hers. "If I find out the contrary, your life will be forfeit," he said, vanishing into smoke.

In his insubstantial state, he watched the Guardian drop to her hands and knees, coughing so hard that she eventually vomited all over the floor. She collected herself and got to her feet, stumbling to one of the back bedrooms. He followed her through the ether, watching as she went to the far side of the bed and pushed on a section of the wall. A hidden door popped open, revealing a wall safe with a number keypad. She punched in a ten-digit code and the safe door released. As soon as it was open, he pulled out of the ether and rematerialized just feet away from her, simultaneously calling upon the hellfire with full strength. The Guardian screamed as she burned and when she was dead, he stepped toward her body and pulled a little black velvet drawstring bag from the confines of the small vault.

Opening the bag, he smiled at the object of his obsession, a small rust-colored rock. Its etchings were barely visible in the dim light of dawn.

"Now only the waxing moon stands between me and my goal. Thank you, Guardian. You've been most helpful."

He pulled the drawstrings of the bag together, once again concealing the stone, and tucked the bag into his coat pocket. As he turned to walk out of the apartment, two words ran through his mind.

Devil's Island.

CHAPTER TWENTY-SEVEN

Michael

The three vampires stood at the ready to help her the moment she snapped out of the memory. Michael and Lucas had explained what Deziree's sessions were like. Michael was prepared for the choking, coughing, and even the stomach sickness. But this vision seemed to be more intense than her previous connections. At one point, her body seemed to be seizing but it only lasted a few moments.

Deziree's body finally relaxed slightly and she slowly raised her head, her eyes closed. Suddenly, her eyes snapped open and they were completely black. A sickening grin spread across her face.

"So this is what she's been up to." The voice was not Deziree's, but that of a male. She looked around at the three stunned vampires, slowly shaking her head. "Tsk, tsk, parasites. You shouldn't play with things you don't understand." Then her whole body went limp and she slumped to the ground.

"What the Hell was that!" Kade cried, stumbling backward

Michael caught Deziree and cradled her in his arms. "Dez! Dez! Wake up! Can you hear me?" He was frantic with worry, afraid she might not live through this encounter.

Then her eyes fluttered open.

"Vegas," she said huskily, one that was, thankfully, her own, "can you please stop shaking me? I think I'm going to hurl."

"Oh thank the gods," he said with relief. "I thought you were dead."

"Nope," she said, trying to pull herself to a sitting position, "not dead, but I imagine this is what it feels like."

Michael chuckled and helped her to her feet.

"Okay. Explain. You said she sees visions. You didn't say anything about voices and crazy demon faces," Kade said, crossing his arms.

"Faces? Voices? Did I talk during the vision?" Deziree asked, thoroughly puzzled.

"The demon," Michael explained. "He linked with you somehow. He spoke to us."

"Wait. You guys could *hear* him?" Slight panic tainted her voice.

"I think he possessed you," Lucas answered. "Your eyes went black as night. It was the creepiest thing I have ever seen."

"He knows what we are up to now," Michael said with a sigh.

"It doesn't matter," Dez replied. "He gave us what we needed. Right before I left the vision, he thought the location of the gateway. Ever heard of a place called Devil's Island?"

CHAPTER TWENTY-EIGHT

Dez

"Here it is. Devil's Island is a name commonly used to refer to an old French penal colony down off the coast of French Guiana," Vegas read from the computer screen. After they finished at the West Village apartment, he had kept true to his word and they'd gone straight back to her apartment. Vegas had made her a cup of hot chocolate while she took a lengthy shower. Once she was in comfortable clothes and bundled in a blanket, he brought her laptop into the living room so they could discuss their plan.

"So, we know where we are going," Lucas said. "When do we leave?"

"He said something to the effect of all that stands between him and his goal is the moon." Deziree tried recalling the exact words he'd used, but clearly the demon had messed with her mind while he'd been in there. Details were hazy.

"The full moon. I think the next one is in a week or so," Vegas said, clicking through webpages.

"Not even," Kade replied. "It's three days away."

"It makes sense," Dez replied. "A lot of magicks are

done at the full moon. Witches draw their power from it. Asmodeus is just one demon. He's going to need all the juice he can get to pull this off."

"You even know this thing's name?" Kade asked in surprise.

"Oh," Dez said with a sarcastic laugh, "yeah, you missed the big reveal in London. This demon happens to be the bastard who fathered me. Don't worry though. We've already been over this. The first chance I get to put a bullet through his eye, I won't hesitate to pull the trigger. I have no love for daddy dearest."

"I did *not* see that coming," Kade muttered.

"Don't feel bad," she replied. "None of us did. I had no idea myself. When we knew a demon was on our plane, I wasn't exactly thinking it would be a long-lost relative. As to the *when* in this little equation, if the full moon is in just a few days, I say we use the next two to rest up and possibly look into getting some back up. Then we can head south and put a stop to this thing."

"Our first plan should involve intercepting this guy before he can get to Devil's Island. If we can kill him before he gets there, he can't open the gateway," said Vegas.

"And if that fails?" Lucas asked.

"We'll have to tell Cassandra," Kade said.

"No, not yet. Not until we know who the conspirators are. The whole thing could fall apart if the traitor finds out. If I tell her what's going on, she would be suspicious. The traitor would pick up on her change in attitude," Dez said. "I'm supposed to call her. Maybe I can convince her to give me more information about the gateway without letting on to her exactly what we're doing."

"It's worth a try," Kade said.

"When we discover the traitor, we can bring them before the Council. Until then, we'll do our best to handle this on our own," Dez said, leaning back against the comfortable couch cushions.

They continued to read up on Devil's Island until Deziree caught herself nodding off on the couch. Vegas gently shook her shoulder.

"Hey, you're snoring. Why don't you go to bed?" he suggested.

She nodded drowsily. "Good idea," she said, standing. She turned to walk down the hallway but stopped, turning to Kade. "Are you staying?"

"No, I am going to go back to my place," he replied. "I have people waiting to hear from me. Call when you wake up. I'm organizing a meeting with my coven to assemble a team for South America." Kade took Dez's hand in his and kissed her knuckles. "Get some rest. I'll see you tomorrow." After his goodbyes were through, he left quickly.

Lucas stretched out and yawned. "I'm turning in too," he said.

"The spare bedroom is all yours." Dez pulled her blanket tighter around herself. She turned to Vegas and asked, "Are you ready for bed?"

A mischievous light filled his eyes as he smiled. "Very ready."

"Keep it down in there!" Lucas called after them.

CHAPTER TWENTY-NINE

"Close the door, please," she requested, dropping the throw blanket she'd been wrapped in at the end of her bed. He detected something unsettling in her voice.

"What's wrong?" he asked.

"I am going to show you something and I don't want you to freak out. I need you to know that I would never hurt you."

"Hurt me?" he asked, chuckling. "I don't think you'd hurt me."

"Sit down." Again, he did as she asked. She shut her eyes for a moment and when she opened them back up, she stared at him. "Do you feel it?"

"Feel wh—" His words were cut off. He doubled over at a rush of pain in his abdomen, then looked up at her in shock.

She released the pull of the hellfire and a tear streaked down her cheek.

"I'm so sorry," she said, falling to her knees in front of him, more tears streaking down her face. "I don't know when it started. I just woke up and could *feel* the ability there."

"You have the power to call hellfire," he stammered, totally aghast and disarmed.

"I'm sorry," she said. "I feel terrible for hurting you. I'll never ever use it. I won't ..." She buried her face in his neck. "I don't know why this is happening. It's like he's changing me, like connecting to those memories has made me more like him. I don't want to be *anything* like him."

She was obviously terrified. Dez wasn't one for outward displays of emotion, never mind full-on crying jags. He couldn't remember ever seeing her this upset or scared in all the time they'd known each other.

"No," Michael said, putting her at arm's length. "Look at me, Dez." He locked eyes with her. "You are *not* like him. No matter how many times you get into his head, you're still you. You may be a little different, but you are still Dez. Don't ever forget that. "Who knows, you've probably had the power in you this whole time and didn't know it. It's not like you were ever pushed to embrace your demon side. Maybe simply not accessing it suppressed it."

"We don't know for sure," she said, wiping her eyes. Vegas pulled her into a tight hug.

"I can prove it," he said, releasing her and striding toward the door. He opened it and craned his neck into the hallway. "Lucas," he called quietly. "Come here, please."

Dez heard footsteps coming down the hall and then Lucas spoke up. "If you guys are about to ask me to join in, let me just say now, I am *not* interested. He's my brother, and you're Deziree, and that would just be all kinds of weird."

"Get in here," Vegas said, tugging him by the arm. "Read her."

"Her aura? Sure." Lucas looked at her for a moment and then said, "Your aura is black but saturated with purple. As though someone took watered down roofing tar and mixed it with an equal amount of purple glitter."

"Is it getting darker?" she asked.

"I won't lie to you, it has gotten darker over the last few days, but the purple has also become deeper, more mixed in. Almost like it was oil and water before and recently, they've found a way to blend and become one."

"See?" Vegas asked. "You're not one of them. You're different. I know it; Lucas can actually *see* it."

"What's this all about?" Lucas asked.

Vegas looked at Dez, letting her know it was up to her to tell if she wanted to. She appreciated knowing he wouldn't tell anyone, even his own brother, without her permission.

"I can control hellfire." Saying it out loud made her feel a little better, like she didn't have anything to hide.

"Seriously?" he asked.

She nodded.

"Think of it this way: now you'll save a ton of money on ammunition," Lucas said with a grin.

Dez grabbed a throw pillow from her bed and launched it at Lucas's head. He ducked just in time and it flew past him into the hall.

"Thanks, Lucas," Vegas said, shaking his head. "Now go get some rest."

Lucas left the room and Vegas closed the door behind him.

"See? No worries," Vegas said brightly. Dez climbed into the bed and once she was tucked underneath the comforter, Vegas turned off the overhead light, leaving only the glow of the side table lamps to illuminate the room.

He rummaged through his suitcase and changed into a comfortable pair of sweatpants. When he climbed into bed, he turned off the bedside lamp and Deziree had trouble remembering why she wanted to go to sleep. She rolled over to face him, briefly marveling at the handsome face she never got tired of looking at. She lifted her head so he could lay his arm out for her to use as a pillow and she contentedly curled up in his arms. As she drifted off to sleep, she almost thought she heard him whisper *I love you.* It didn't matter if he had said it or not, she smiled at the beauty of the sentiment. She found through all this, through all the questions and the terror... She loved him too.

CHAPTER THIRTY

Dez

The next morning, Deziree woke up to the aroma of coffee and bacon. She'd slept in later than normal and if those smells hadn't been lingering in the air, she probably would have been hard pressed to drag herself out of bed. Her growling stomach demanded food. She swung her legs over the side of the bed and made her way to the kitchen.

"Good morning," she said in the middle of a yawn. Both vampires were sitting at the breakfast bar, sipping coffee with empty plates in front of them. She gave Vegas a kiss on the cheek as she walked behind him.

"Good morning," he replied, not looking up from the laptop screen where he was doing more research.

"Breakfast smells amazing," she said, pouring herself a cup of coffee at the counter behind him.

"There's plenty here," Lucas said, thumbing through news headlines on his phone. "I think I may have made too much."

"No, sir. You can never have too much bacon," she said, shoveling a stack of it onto her plate. "I could eat a whole pig right now."

She glanced up at Vegas and smiled. He turned to smile back at her but he jolted backward, bumping his coffee mug and spilling its contents on the counter. Lucas jumped, so startled he dropped his phone.

"Dez, sweetie. Have you looked in the mirror yet today?" Vegas asked.

"No, I came out here as soon as I smelled the coffee. What's wrong with my face, do I have wrinkle lines from the pillow?" she asked, stepping away from the counter to look in a mirror hanging in her living room.

"Holy shit!" she yelped, jumping back from her own reflection. Her normal crystal blue irises looked like spheres of black glass. "What ... what the hell is wrong with my eyes?" she yelled hysterically at no one in particular.

"Just ... just calm down, Dez," Vegas said, trying his best to placate her.

"Calm down?" she screamed. "Really? Calm down? *Look at my eyes*! I look like a strung out rat!"

She turned and ran for her bedroom. Turning on the lights above her vanity mirror, she looked at her eyes again. She opened her eyes as far as she could with her fingers, examining them up close. She was a little relieved to find they were not *completely* black. The irises still had flecks of blue scattered throughout the black space. She closed her eyes and breathed deep. She heard Vegas enter the room and close the door.

"Dez," he whispered.

She shushed him and he went silent, sitting on the corner of the bed. She breathed and concentrated, willing her eyes to change back to their normal color. *Breathe in. Breathe out. Breathe in. Breathe out.* She opened her eyes and was once again looking at the familiar pale blue she was used to. She heaved a sigh of relief.

"What the hell was that?" she muttered. She kept

staring at her eyes in the mirror, terrified they'd turn black if she dared look away again.

"Something else we will have to grow accustomed to, I suspect." He walked up behind her and laid a hand on her shoulder. Their eyes met in the mirror. "You didn't look like a strung out rat."

"I didn't feel any different."

"I bet it's just like hellfire. Maybe it's just another one of your undiscovered powers." He was rubbing her shoulders, hoping to relieve some of her tension. Seeing her eyes hadn't blackened after a few minutes made her feel better. She sighed again, trying to will away her stress.

"Now I really do need coffee."

Vegas ushered her back into the kitchen. Lucas had cleaned up the spilled coffee and refilled his and Vegas's mugs. He had gone back to his newsfeed as if nothing had happened. She figured he would have had a snide remark to make, but he hadn't said anything.

"Would you like some cheese?" he offered with a smile, batting his eyes in mock innocence.

And there it is, she thought.

CHAPTER THIRTY-ONE

Dez

After breakfast, Deziree made her planned phone call to Cassandra. The time difference from New York to Venice wasn't a problem as it was only a matter of six hours. New York's 11:38 AM was only early evening for them.

Rather than sitting in pajamas all day, she multitasked, putting Cassandra on speakerphone while she dressed.

"Deziree," she greeted, "how are you, dear?"

"I'm well," she responded. "We are back in New York at the moment."

"Were you able to find anything?"

"Unfortunately, no." *I'm going to Hell for this.* "We haven't had any sightings of the demon either. I have no clue where it is and nothing to go on." Deziree was careful to cover up as much as she knew as possible. She hated the thought of dragging Cassandra into this mess any further than she already was. She could only be in one place at a time and as long as that was true, she couldn't always protect Cassandra. Not knowing the traitor's identity severely limited the amount of information she could divulge.

"Well," Cassandra said with a sigh, "thank you for trying anyway. It's more than some around here are doing. Everyone is spending all of their time gossiping about the whole thing and none of it trying to come up with a solution. Each coven has people out looking for anyone with black eyes, but the demon could simply wear sunglasses to disguise that feature. Without knowing where it is going or what it looks like, our hands are pretty well tied."

At the mention of the demon's black eyes, a knot formed in the pit of Deziree's stomach. She wished she could confide in Cassandra over all the changes she was going through.

"At least people are looking," she finally said. "It's better than doing nothing." Deziree tried to think of a crafty way to segue into asking about how to close the gate but couldn't come up with anything clever. Instead, she chose the direct method. "Hey, I have a question for you."

"Of course, dear. Ask away."

"Say we aren't able to stop the demon in time to prevent him from opening the gateway. What then? I mean, you said it takes blood to close it. What exactly did you mean?"

"A sacrifice," Cassandra replied. "However, you can't just throw any poor soul into the gateway. That would be far too easy. This may sound harsh, but if that were the case, we'd just jailbreak the worst criminal in existence and use him or her. The spell requires a sacrifice born out of love. The person must willingly spill their blood and give up their life in the name of love."

"Who made the sacrifice when you closed the gate before?"

Cassandra was quiet for a moment. When she answered, her voice was laced with regret. "Adamo Riccetti gave himself to close the gate. Adamo was a good boy, an enthusiastic witch. He was also madly in love with your mother. She was just a couple of years older than he was, but it didn't stop him from following her around like a little lost puppy dog. He had gone to visit her under one false pretense or another. Everyone knew the real reason: Adamo dreamed of one day making Catalina his bride. He just never mustered up the nerve to tell her how he felt. As he told it, he arrived at her home that evening and knocked on her door. Rather than her usual warmth, he was greeted with Catalina's terrified screams. He opened the door and found her on her floor, her face beaten and bloody. Her clothes were torn and she was shaking violently. We still don't know why the demon left her alive that night. Three days later, Adamo volunteered to be the sacrifice. Catalina was so damaged from her attack, he knew there was no chance of them being together. Rather than watch it happen to more people around him, spending the rest of his days mourning what could have been, he chose to give his life. He loved your mother deeply and sacrificed himself because of that love. When we were ready, he joined us when we went to the open gateway. After they spoke the blood oath incantation with the stone, he cut a line across his palm and simply walked into the gate. The moment his body made contact with the gateway's energy, it started to seal. It looked as if someone were quickly mending the tear between realities with a needle and thread."

"Did my mother love him back?" Dez asked.

"I think so," Cassandra replied. "I'm not sure his sacrifice would have worked if she hadn't. They would have made a good match too. They were both so sweet and caring. Had the demons not punched their way through into our realm, I imagine they probably would have had a long and happy life together surrounded by their sons, daughters, and lots of grandchildren."

The line was quiet for a long moment, and then

Cassandra continued. Deziree checked her clothes for wrinkles, smoothing her hands over her blouse.

"Your mother really was a good woman, Deziree," Cassandra said. "She had a kind heart. I wish you could have known each other."

Dez never talked about her mother. It wasn't due to strong emotions on the subject. It was due to a complete lack thereof. The day Deziree had been born, her mother refused to even look at her. Being born the bastard child of a demon to a woman who was an unwilling party in the conception hadn't allowed her mother to see her as anything more than a monster. Cassandra had taken her in when she was only a few hours old, hiring wet nurses to handle the care she was unable to give being a vampire. By the time she was old enough to understand Cass wasn't actually her mother, her biological mother was long gone, having died by suicide soon after Deziree was born.

She harbored no ill feelings toward the woman. Catalina had been broken in the worst possible way and was unable to come back from it. Through Deziree's entire life, Cassandra had been the only mother she had ever known, and she didn't bother wasting time crying over a woman she had never met.

"I do too," Dez admitted, "but I think I got a pretty good substitute out of the deal."

"Oh thank you, dear. I tried to do the best I could, given the circumstances."

"Well, I think you did a wonderful job." Deziree busied herself with applying light layers of makeup to her face. "Hey, I have to get going. I am going to go check on things at Onyx today. I need to make sure no one burned the place down while I have been gone. I will talk to you soon, okay?"

"Very good," Cassandra replied. "Talk to you soon."

Deziree went out into the living room where the men waited for her.

"Did you guys get all of that?" she asked, dropping herself on to the couch.

"We did," Vegas answered. "So if we can't stop this guy ahead of time, the only way to close the gateway is a sacrifice grounded in love."

"Yes, sir," she affirmed. "That means the only option is to stop Asmodeus because a sacrifice is out of the question. I don't care what it takes. That is *not* happening. Got it?"

"Loud and clear," Lucas responded. "Can I ask one question?"

"Shoot."

"How exactly do you plan on closing the gateway if he manages to get it open? And also, what about the things that end up coming out of it?"

"That's two questions, but both have the same answer," she told him. "I don't know. We will just have to make sure it doesn't get that far."

CHAPTER THIRTY-TWO

Dez

That evening, Deziree went to Onyx. The whole way there, she silently prayed her car was alright. The night she stayed with Vegas, they had walked to his brownstone rather than driving and her custom 1951 Mercury Coupe had been sitting there for the last week. She was sure Jack wouldn't let anything happen to it, but that didn't stop her from picturing some punk kid, late at night, deciding it would be funny to rake a fistful of keys across the hood leaving jagged scars in the dark, cherry red paint, effectively ruining the beautiful dark purple ghostly flames. The more she thought about it, the more she wished the cab driver would step on it.

When they finally pulled into the parking lot, she paid the driver quickly and all but sprinted to her car. She inspected it for scratches or other damage. She was happy to find the Merc was exactly as she'd left it. Satisfied, she crossed the street to Onyx. The door was unlocked.

The bar was dark but Dez could hear someone moving around in the storeroom. She knew it was still much too early for the staff to be there.

"Hello?" she called out. She heard a crashing noise and then Jack's familiar voice.

Jack appeared at the storeroom door carrying two full boxes of liquor. "Oh hey. You're back. You're back kind of early. How was your vacation?" he asked.

"Terrible. I'm taking a real one in a few weeks. What are you doing here so early?"

He set the boxes down on the bar top, not looking the least bit strained by the weight he had just been carrying.

"The last week here has been insane," he said. "I have been double stocking the speed bars for the last three nights. The bar alone has been raking in about five grand a night."

"Not that I am complaining, but why?" The sudden spike in business was good for her bank account, but their usual take in a night was between two and three thousand dollars.

"I started asking around and it turns out that two shifter joints here in town got shut down last week, for, get this, 'health code violations.' Apparently the places were really nasty. I guess the other clubs in town don't exactly welcome shifters with open arms."

"Any problems with security?" she asked.

"Nope," he replied. "I asked Maxwell to double the staff he's sending here. We have plenty of muscle to go around but we haven't really needed it. Everyone has done really well at keeping their cool."

"Good. Well, I'm heading up to take care of a few things. Pop in if you need something," she said. He cordially saluted her with two fingers and continued stocking the bars. She climbed the stairs to her office.

Deziree sat down at her desk and pulled out her phone. She'd texted Charlie just to see how he'd been doing but had received no reply. Finding it odd that he hadn't answered her message, she decided to call him. It didn't ring. She immediately got an automated message.

The number you have reached is no longer in service. Please check your number and dial again.

She had three numbers for him in her contact list and tried the second one. She received the same result. She looked at her phone's screen skeptically, then swiped to the third number. She had only ever dialed the third number in his contact file once before. That number was reserved for extreme emergencies. The one time she had used it, she and Charlie had a close call at a job and had gotten separated.

This time, although it wasn't an extreme emergency, worry escalated her need to speak with him.

"Screw it." She tapped the number in the contact file and hit dial.

The line rang twice before it clicked and a gruff man's voice answered. She'd spoken with this same man the last and only other time she'd called the number.

"Yeah?" he said with his long, southern drawl.

"Hi, I am looking for Charlie. Have you seen him?"

"No Charlie here," he replied abruptly before he ended the call.

Deziree stared at her phone in disbelief. *The son of a bitch hung up on me!* She hit redial and waited.

The gruff voice answered again. "Yeah?"

"Don't hang up!" she snapped into the phone. "I am looking for Charlie and you helped me locate him once before. Can you please tell me how to get a hold of him or pass a message on to him for me?"

There was a long pause and then he sighed.

"Look," the man let out a sigh, "Charlie is gone and he don't wanna be found. Whatever business you got with him, just let it go, you hear?"

"I've been a friend of his for a long time."

"Miss," he said, "if you been a friend of his for a long time, then you should know when Charlie sets his mind to somethin', ain't nothin' gonna change it. All I knows is he told me if anyone called lookin' for him, then to tell them I ain't never heard of him. He's off the grid. Now, I got my own business to attend to. You take care now."

The line went dead and Deziree sat at her desk, completely dumbfounded.

"He really did it," she said to herself.

Charlie had really sworn off his old life to be with the mystery woman he was so smitten with. He had committed himself to spending the rest of his life living under the radar all for the sake of love. She couldn't help but admire him for it. There was no reason she couldn't be with Vegas if Charlie could be with his lady.

Vegas. Even though so much had changed in her life since the demon business had started, he remained the only loyal constant. She'd never thought being in anyone's arms could feel so right. Kissing him felt warm and familiar. Being with him was where she belonged and she knew it. She wondered why and how they'd spent so long without each other. Why had she ever chosen loneliness over what she felt with him? *We'll never have to feel that again.* She smiled to herself and then something dawned on her.

"Great," she muttered. "Now I have to find a new explosives guy."

On her way home, Deziree took a detour to a nearby synagogue. Earlier that afternoon, Vegas and Lucas had left to track down something of the liquid variety to eat and she had taken the opportunity to do a little digging on the computer. When she ran her search, she had been amazed at the sheer number of websites regarding demons. A great many of them were directly related to video games, but buried in the search results, she had found some information she thought might be helpful.

Demonic possession, Dez knew, was real. However, the media had sensationalized possession. The general population either didn't believe in it or believed it to be something far more theatrical than it really was. All around the world there were priests and rabbis who legitimately performed exorcisms, quiet ritualized ceremonies in which they would force the demon out of the victim's body and back through the veil into Hell. The victims' families almost always held vigil, waiting with bated breath to hear whether or not their loved one survived the cleansing. Exorcisms were somber events which often resulted in the victim leaving the room in a body bag.

There were also a great many men and women in the world masquerading as healers, with their traveling tent revivals, taking the money of people who could not afford to give. Those men and women were frauds, preying on people who had very real problems, problems having nothing at all to do with demons. Alcoholics, adulterers, and drug addicts would all gather around in hopes the preacher would expel the demon from their bodies, enabling them to lead a good and wholesome life again. Gambling addicts were dragged in to be "cured," only to throw their money away in another gamble by financing those false organizations. Those people were crooks and deserved to be kicked in the teeth.

Rabbi Sachs did not sound like one of those people.

The man had become somewhat of an underground legend. Several pages into her search results, she had found a number of websites all claiming to contain real images and videos of exorcisms. Among those pages were many articles about a mysterious Rabbi Sachs in Manhattan, who many claimed was the real thing. She had read through the articles one by one, and in the end, found the account of a man who had been at the exorcism of his little sister.

After being told by several doctors their daughter suffered from nothing more than mental illness, his parents had finally turned to their rabbi. The man writing the article explained that upon hearing the story of his sister, the rabbi didn't hesitate for one moment and insisted they bring him to the girl. Once there, he confirmed she was in fact possessed by a demon, but stated that judging by the rotten smell saturating their home, the girl was dead already and nothing could be done to help her. The family begged him to do something. They told him they could not bear to continue seeing their daughter in that condition. He obliged and for fourteen hours, he performed the prayers and rituals to rid her body of the demonic entity. The man stated he had sat beside the rabbi the entire time and saw many things that convinced him, beyond a shadow of a doubt, the thing sitting in front of him was no longer his sister. He said her eyes had even turned black as night at one point.

When he finally gave up, the rabbi told the family he would be unable to rid the body of the demon as there was no soul present to save. Their daughter was nothing more than an empty shell and they needed to look at other options. He explained to them there was a way to finally put their daughter to rest. His solution to their situation was what brought Dez to his synagogue.

She walked up to the visitor door on the side of the building and knocked. The viewing hatch opened and quickly closed again. She heard the release of two locks and then the door slid open. He was a small, olive skinned man. He was shorter than she was and dressed conservatively in a white, button-down shirt and a pair of black dress pants. His yarmulke rested on a thin swath of dark brown curls.

"Can I help you?" he asked, his raspy voice betraying the cigarette habit Dez could smell on him.

"Yes," she responded, "I'm looking for Rabbi Sachs. Is he here?"

"May I ask who's looking for him?"

"Oh, of course. My name is Deziree Davanzati. I'm here to ask him some questions about his exorcism practices."

He eyed her suspiciously for a moment and then spoke. "And what exactly would a demon want with that particular piece of information?"

Deziree quirked a brow.

"I could smell it on you the minute I opened the door. Although, I must admit, you don't smell like all the other demons I've encountered." He looked at her expectantly, an eyebrow raised.

"I'm half. My father was a demon."

"Ah," he said. "Interesting."

"What are you?" she asked.

"Very good at my job," he fired back without hesitation.

"Well, you smell different from most holy men I've encountered, so I assume you're Rabbi Sachs," she said sarcastically, chuckling.

"I am. But I have to wonder what you're doing here. You know what I do. What could you possibly want with me?"

"I have a bit of a situation. Is there a place we can speak in private?"

"Experience has taught me what to do with your kind, even if you are only half. I suggest you don't try anything with me," he said, wiping his forehead.

"We're on the same side," she said, holding up her hands as if to surrender to his demand.

"Very well," he said, "follow me please." He stood back, motioning for her to come in. Deziree took a deep breath and stepped through the doorway.

CHAPTER THIRTY-THREE

Michael

Michael and Lucas returned to Deziree's apartment and found her sitting on the couch, cradling a box of bullets. She was loading her black and silver Heckler and Koch USP 45.

"Most girls spend their time doing girly things like painting their toenails," Lucas said. "Yours cuddles with ammunition and firearms."

Deziree smiled wide and said, "I have presents for you boys."

"Presents?" Michael asked.

"Yes," she said excitedly as she slipped the last bullet into the magazine, "presents." She pushed the mag into the handle of the gun and released the slide. She double checked to make sure the safety was on, then set aside her effects. She grabbed her dark green messenger bag off of the floor. She produced two boxes of bullets, giving each vampire his own. She grinned as if she were a five year old again and had just made them each a macaroni picture.

"Bullets. You shouldn't have," Michael said monotonically.

"Not just any bullets!" she exclaimed. "Special bullets. Compliments of my new friend, Rabbi Jacob Sachs."

"You made a friend?" Michael asked.

Deziree told them the story of the exorcism she read about. "He's not exactly a traditional rabbi. His solution for getting rid of the demon was to pump it full of bullets wiped down with a cloth soaked in holy water. He said one bullet won't do it. A single shot will certainly slow it down, but he had to shoot the girl nine times to kill the demon."

"He shot an innocent girl?" Lucas asked, obviously shocked by the rabbi's choice of action.

"He shot a girl's *body*," Deziree clarified. "The girl was already dead. The demon had killed her long before he got to her. It set up shop in her body. He thinks this could help us. It may not kill Asmodeus, but it may buy us the time we need to stop him. If we can get enough rounds into him before he can begin performing the ritual, we may actually be able to stop this thing." Deziree was back to grinning at the two of them.

"This could actually work," Michael said. "I'll have to get my guns from my place."

"No need," Deziree said as she ran down the hallway. When she returned from her bedroom, she was carrying two more guns identical to her own. They eyed the .45s when handed them.

"Geez, Dez," Lucas said, examining the hand gun. "How many of these do you have?"

"Four," she replied. "I had two here, one at the club, and one in the glove box of the Merc. I also have plenty of spare mags and a few belts that hold three each. We will have more than enough fire power on us."

"And how do you suppose we are going to get all of this through airport security?" Lucas asked. "Am I right to assume these weapons are not legally registered?"

Michael smiled, kissed Deziree on the cheek and said, "Let's call Kade."

"In a minute," Dez replied with a wry smile, then draped herself over Michael's shoulders. She pressed her lips against his, smiling throughout the engrossing kiss. For a moment, they forgot about everything in the world around them. He surrendered, allowing himself to get lost in the moment. When she ended the kiss, it took him a moment to clear the daze from his mind.

"Gross," Lucas said, averting his eyes. "I'm just gonna go."

"What was that for?" he asked, searching her beautiful blue eyes for what had changed.

"I found out today that Charlie is gone," she explained. "He is an immortal and yet he chose to be with a mortal. He's doomed. He's going to suffer through watching her grow old and he knows full well he's going to lose her, but he loved her enough to put himself through it anyway. Finding out he went underground to live with her made me realize how lucky I am. The news about Charlie got me thinking about Lucas and Natalia. He had her in his life so briefly and yet he wouldn't trade the time he had with her for anything." She gently wiped the lip gloss off his lips, then looked him in the eyes. "I want you to know I am in this. I want that kind of love. I want a love that makes you willing to give up the world to have it for as long as you can. No more walls. No more emotional barricades. I am in this and I am not going anywhere."

Michael had no idea how to answer, so he kissed her sweetly and briefly instead. Deziree had always been so reserved when it came to expressing any kind of emotion. She was just like him in that regard.

"I'm in this too," he replied. They both had some learning to do, that was for sure.

"Good," she said, squeezing him tighter. Then she released her grip. "Now call Kade and get the ball rolling."

Kade arrived at Deziree's apartment a few hours later with the news they had been hoping for.

"I have arranged for a private plane to fly us in to Paramaribo, Suriname," he explained. "We will be landing on the private estate of a friend. He's out of the country on business, but he has instructed his people to provide us with transport from the estate to Cayenne, French Guiana. His estate is not far from the border. Once we're there, it's up to us to get to Devil's Island, but it shouldn't be a problem. Unfortunately, this means our schedule is bumped up. The extra days we had to get down there will be spent traveling."

"When do we leave?" Michael asked.

Kade looked at his watch and replied, "In approximately two hours."

"You managed to get a private plane arranged at this hour?" Michael asked. It was the middle of the night and, vampire dealings or not, arranging a private plane in the darkest hours of night on a whim was quite the feat.

"It took me pulling some strings and calling in some favors but yes, we are all set to go."

"Alright," Michael said, turning to Lucas and Deziree, "pack your bags." They each headed for their rooms and Michael turned back to Kade. "Will any of your people be joining us for this trip?"

"They are going to meet us in French Guiana," Kade replied. "They're all flying out tomorrow."

"How many?"

"Six. I decided not to call together the coven after all and ended up hand-picking a select team instead. From the sound of things, we may not even need them. We just need to get close enough to the demon to put him down."

"That's true," Michael said, "but I would rather have some back up and not need them than have no one and end up in way over our heads. Thank you. It really means the world to us that you and your people are doing this."

"Think nothing of it," Kade replied. "In cases like this, we're not covens, races, countries, or species. We're citizens of the realm. We're all each other's people. We all have to fight this. Now, let's go take care of this demon," he said with a smirk, patting Vegas's shoulder emphatically.

CHAPTER THIRTY-FOUR

Dez

Half a day later, the three vampires and half demon arrived in Cayenne, French Guiana. They checked into the Novotel Cayenne hotel and went to their rooms to get settled. Kade's six men were due to arrive later in the night.

Deziree set her suitcases by the door and stripped off her clothes, piece by piece, leaving a trail from the door to the bed. She pulled back the covers and crawled into the comfort of the sheets. She had left Vegas, Lucas, and Kade talking in the hallway. She was so tired, the only thing she could concentrate on was how good the pillow waiting for her was going to feel. The minute she pulled the covers up to her chin, she felt the pull of sleep stealing her consciousness. As the darkness took her, she allowed her mind to drift. The last thought she remembered having was one of anxiety over the task ahead of them.

Deziree stood in a black void. There was no sky above her. There was no ground below her. Just a black space of nothingness. The lack of reference point in the space was very disorientating. She knew in the back of her mind she was dreaming, but she had never experienced a dream like this before.

She turned around, spinning in a slow circle, expecting something to appear — a memory, an illusion, something — but nothing happened. The silence of the space was deafening. Her ears began to ring from the startling lack of noise.

She shut her eyes and concentrated, trying to will something familiar to appear, Onyx or her apartment. She even tried to conjure the shower she and Vegas had shared. She forced her mind to study every detail of the memory in an effort to make it materialize in her dream and that's when his voice cracked through the silence.

"Dirty little thing, aren't you?"

Deziree's eye snapped open, and standing just a few feet away from her was Asmodeus. He wore a black, three-piece suit, the elegant cut of which contrasted with his true, ugly nature. On anyone else, the suit would have been attractive. On him it looked completely wrong.

"I didn't think I'd see you here," Dez said.

"You must have known we'd inevitably meet again," Asmodeus said with a smirk. "Just like the humans you're trying to protect know their inevitable end is coming."

"Humans expecting Hell to spill into their realm? I don't think so," she said, shaking her head.

"'Apocalypse!' 'The end is near!' Those are their words, not ours, but they do fit, don't they? They know their end is coming, no matter what name they give it. They continue to pray to a god who abandoned them long ago, believing their faith is enough to save them. Even after several millennia, they are still ignorant enough to believe their god is the only one. He's just one of many who got bored with their playthings and left long ago. But not before banishing my kind to a realm of never-ending misery for nothing more than challenging the merits of the humans' existence. For *them*."

Utter disgust dripped from his every word. Of the many gods that have existed for millions of years, the one that a large portion of the globe still worshipped was the one that created the Hell dimension. Following an uprising in his own dimension, a handful of angels were banished from his realm and cast into a new world to suffer alone for all of eternity. Religions around the world tweaked the story here and changed a detail there, but the truth was, humans weren't to blame. It was basically a cosmic power play gone wrong. From the sound of things, demons were sore losers.

"You guys are seriously still hanging onto that grudge?" she asked. "The humans didn't do that to you."

"Why do you defend them? They don't care about anything but themselves. It's why the old gods abandoned them. The gods weren't forgotten, they were discarded by an ungrateful creation. The very beings that weaved this universe into existence can't be bothered to save them. Why do you feel compelled to do so?"

"I'm tied to them," she said, considering letting the truth rip.

"Tied to them how?" he sneered. "Have you fallen in love with one of their kind?"

"You haven't figured it out yet? No, I suppose you're too busy plotting the destruction of the world, a plan which will *fail*, by the way. Don't you feel something when we're close together, or are you too busy raping human women to feel anything?"

"Raping human women?" He may never have thought of his victims after their crimes had been perpetrated. She

153

could tell her words had forced him to dig deep. His black eyes fixed on her but he remained silent for a moment before continuing. "I suppose you're the unfortunate offspring of a demon-human copulation."

She tipped her head and shrugged her shoulders.

"You're not mine, are you?" He chuckled. "Oh that's rich!" She let her silence do the talking. "This is going to be fun." With his final words, he vanished from the void and another voice broke through.

CHAPTER THIRTY-FIVE

Michael

Michael gently shook Deziree's shoulder. He had come into the room the night before only to find her in such a deep sleep she never even stirred when he crawled into the bed with her. He had decided to just let her sleep until it was time to get ready to leave. Now that they were ready to leave for the island, he was having trouble waking her.

"Dez," he said, placing a kiss on her cheek. "It's time to get up."

She finally started to come out of her near-comatose state and he breathed a small sigh of relief. She stretched and groaned her displeasure at having to wake up. She blinked her eyes at the brightness of the sun streaming in through the windows.

"You must have been wiped. You've been out for about nineteen hours straight."

"How is that possible?" she asked, rubbing her eyes. She sat up and Michael held out a coffee for her. "Thanks."

"The coffee is really good here," he said. "Everyone is

downstairs in the lobby. We'll be ready to go when you are." He kissed her on top of the head and left the room.

❦

Michael found their group sitting in the lobby discussing the travel time to get to the island. Kade had his phone out and was studying the map on the screen.

"We are going to drive from here to Kourou," he explained. "Devil's Island is about fifteen miles off the coast. We could take the ferry, but those tours come back in the afternoon. If we stayed, we would be stranded on the island until the following day. I think it would be best to rent a boat. We'll figure out the details when we reach port."

❦

The group split up between three rental cars. Michael, Lucas, and Deziree were in a car by themselves. Once they were on the road, Deziree told them everything about the dream.

"That explains why you slept for so long," Michael said. "You couldn't come out until he let you. Just one more reason for me to end this guy."

Deziree leaned against Vegas, thinking how incredibly lucky she was to have him in her life as a lover, protector, and partner. She had faith that no matter what happened in the hours to come, he'd be right there by her side.

CHAPTER THIRTY-SIX

Dez

They spent the entire afternoon searching for a boat to rent with no luck. As evening started to settle in, they realized they were running out of time. Kade sent one of his men to scout out a boat they could use. A little over an hour later, he returned indicating he had found a boat big enough for the ten of them. The blue and white cabin cruiser was docked at a vacant vacation home. At thirty feet long, the boat had plenty of room for everyone to be comfortable on the trip out to the island and back. When darkness fell like a shroud on the coast, they hotwired the boat and set off into the choppy surf.

They arrived at the island under full cover of darkness. The tourists were long gone and when Kade shut off the boat's engines, the only sound was that of the ocean waves bumping against the dock and the rocky shore. They climbed out of the boat and followed the path toward the visitor's center.

"I can't see anything," Dez whispered to Vegas, squinting into the salty breeze.

He grasped her hand, entwining his fingers with hers

and replied, "I can see just fine. Stay with me." He guided her up the path leading away from the water. Their group walked in silence, the men scanning their surroundings as they went.

Deziree suddenly felt light-headed. She stopped walking, pulling Vegas to a stop as well.

"What's wrong?" he asked.

"I don't know," she replied. "I feel strange." Deziree tried to look around her and could only make out shadows and outlines. The harder she concentrated on trying to see, the clearer her surroundings became until finally she could see everything as if they were in a muted daylight.

"That's it," Vegas said quietly. "Focus everything you have on it."

Deziree closed her eyes and felt something building deep in her core. She envisioned it as a sphere of energy, humming, increasing in size with every breath she took. She willed it to grow and grow until it filled her whole body, down to her toes and out to her fingertips.

She opened her eyes and it was like seeing the world in a whole new light. Every inch and every detail of the world surrounding her was crystal clear, her sense of sight magnified. What had sounded like eerie silence before was now a cacophony of nature.

"This is amazing," she said, looking all around her. "I can see and hear everything. Is this what it's like for you?"

"Basically," he replied, "but without the black eyes."

She fought the impulse to clap her eyes shut in embarrassment. She still wasn't used to the changes her body had undergone.

"I guess I've got night vision on demand, huh? Another perk of being a half demon. Maybe this isn't such a bad thing. This could come in really handy on my next job."

"Hey, Dez," Lucas said, "Take a big whiff."

Deziree closed her eyes again and inhaled deeply

through her nose, taking in all of the scents around her. She could smell every plant and every flower on the island as if they were right in front of her face. Her eyes snapped open. "Demon. I can smell him. We need to go that way," she said, pointing in the direction of the lighthouse.

"Let's move," Kade said, nodding to his six men.

They came up on the lighthouse and could see a purple glow emanating from behind the weathered stone structure. They crept around until the source of the glow came into view in a clearing well beyond the lighthouse. Asmodeus stood before a shimmering purple orb. The surface undulated and distorted as if something violent was boiling just beneath the surface. A low hum reverberated, growing more intense by the second.

"You're too late!" Asmodeus said, sensing her without seeing her. A glint caught her eye and she noticed he was holding a knife. Before she realized he was moving, he slashed the knife across his hand.

Without hesitation, Deziree started walking toward him, pulled her gun from the small of her back, took a hasty aim, and pulled the trigger. The first shot hit his shoulder, jerking his body to the side. Her second shot missed.

He pulled the Sentinel Stone out of his pocket, placing it in his bleeding palm.

"*Patefacio!*" he boomed. He plunged his hand into the purple glow as Deziree took another shot. This time, the bullet hit its mark, forcing a path through the side of the demon's skull.

Asmodeus's lifeless form dropped to the ground, the hand he had plunged into the roiling sphere was gone, as was the stone. An orange light arced out of the body, hovered in the air and disappeared into the orb.

The hum coming from the sphere suddenly exploded into loud cracks, and a howling wind whipped around them. Bolts of electricity streaked back and forth across the surface. The liquid began to solidify and take shape. Forms from the other side pushed, stretching it as though it were a membrane.

"Get back!" Vegas yelled, barely audible over the deafening noise. They all covered their ears, stepping back and bracing themselves. A terrible tearing noise ripped through the night and screams filled the air.

The gateway was open, a great chasm suspended in the air. Hot wind burst through with hurricane force and the screams grew louder still, transforming into angry shrieks.

The first demon appeared.

A boney, charred hand reached out, grabbed the edge of the portal and pulled, yanking the rest of its body through. It stopped, glanced around, and when its eyes landed on the group, it screamed, its body shaking with fury.

In one fluid motion, Vegas pulled his gun out and fired, hitting the demon in the head with the first shot. The demon dropped from the edge of the portal to the ground and melted into flames of hellfire. The stench of sulfur filled the air.

"Well," he yelled, "that answers that question. Aim for the head and don't miss! We have no idea how many of these things are going to come through."

A roaring erupted from the portal, giving them only a split-second warning before demons issued forth from the gateway. The entire group opened fire, shooting anything that moved. The demons that weren't hit shifted into black smoke and vanished in the wind.

Giant, thundering footsteps rumbled from the chasm, shaking the ground beneath them. Suddenly the gateway ripped wider and out stepped a demon well over nine feet tall. Once he was through the portal, he stood up straight and a pair of massive black tattered wings stretched out from his back.

"Hello again, child."

Asmodeus smiled a feral, toothy grin at Deziree and started toward her.

CHAPTER THIRTY-SEVEN

Dez

"Oh shit," Dez said in a breathy whisper.

"Fire!" Kade yelled.

The sound of gunfire filled the air. Each bullet seemed to do nothing more than infuriate the demon as he stormed towards them. He grabbed one of Kade's men by the throat and ripped his head off.

"Aim for the head!" Vegas shouted as his empty magazine dropped to the sand and he slammed and full one in its place.

They continued to fire at the demon's head as he advanced further, grabbing another of Kade's men, twisting his neck and decapitating him, tossing his body aside like common refuse. Dez hit the release on her gun, dropping the empty mag and shoving another spare into place. She fired at the demon's head repeatedly. Shot after shot, the hail of gunfire seemed to go on forever even though it had probably only been a few minutes.

Finally, the damage they inflicted took a toll. The demon slowed and dropped to one knee, each shot causing his body to jerk. Kade stepped forward and emptied a fresh magazine into Asmodeus's head, and with the last shot, the demon fell to the ground unmoving. The same orange light which had flowed out of his human form now flowed from his demon form, shooting straight into the sky, then it was gone. To be sure he wouldn't get up, they each fired a few more shots into the body and then turned their attention back to the smaller demons advancing on their position.

CHAPTER THIRTY-EIGHT

Lucas

Lucas moved toward the portal, firing his gun at anything that came through. He only hit about every third demon, the rest smoking out before he could fire a shot into them. He glanced toward the rest of the group. They were putting up a good fight, but he knew there was only one way to stop the flow of demons coming into their world.

He looked down at his hand and touched Natalia's ring. He felt it deep in his heart, a certainty: he would never find anyone like her again in his life. He was grateful for the time he had shared with her and would cherish every moment they had together.

He looked back at Michael and Deziree. He was so happy to see his brother finally find love. Having felt that kind of love, even if it was taken away from him prematurely, he couldn't imagine going through an immortal existence without it. He wouldn't allow his brother or Deziree to feel that kind of loss if he could help it. And he could.

He dropped his gun on the ground and advanced toward the gateway. Time seemed to slow with each step he took. The roar of the hot wind coming from the gateway nearly drowned out every other sound. The gunfire faded into the background. He barely heard Michael scream his name. He turned to see his brother running toward him. He held up a hand and shook his head. Michael stopped running and dropped to his knees.

"Somebody has to do it! It may as well be me. I found love and I lost her. You have Dez now. Take care of each other." Lucas gave a small smile and turned back toward the gateway. The sight he saw startled him.

Natalia stood just inside the gateway smiling at him. He blinked, sure his eyes were playing tricks on him. She silently laughed and held her hand out to him. He thumbed the Claddagh ring. He turned, taking one last look at his brother, who was now accompanied by Dez standing beside him, holding his hand.

He expected the vision of Natalia to be gone when he turned back, but she was still standing there, hand outstretched with a smile on her face, her beautifully messy chestnut hair only lightly rustling in spite the heavy wind. He took the last few steps remaining between him and the gateway. *She's waiting for me.* He reached his hand out as he breached the gateway and took hers. When he stepped inside, it was not what he expected. There was no noise. There was no wind. There were no demons. There was only Natalia. He pulled her to him, unable to take his eyes off of her. Their luminescent auras mingled, creating a colorful dance of light around them. He touched his forehead to hers and closed his eyes, savoring the feeling of her in his arms again.

"I've missed you," she whispered.

"I've missed you too," he replied.

The two of them faded into the ether together. Forever.

CHAPTER THIRTY-NINE

Michael

Michael watched helplessly as Lucas's lifeless body slumped to the ground. The moment he made contact with the gateway, a loud crack filled the air and in an instant, the gateway disappeared into nothingness. The dead demons littering the sand were the only evidence it had ever existed. Michael squeezed Deziree's hand as tears fell over his cheeks. His heart ached for the loss of his brother, but he was beyond proud Lucas made the selfless choice, the one which ultimately had saved them all.

He climbed to his feet, wiping the tears from his face. They searched the beach thoroughly, but no other demons were to be found.

"They're gone," Dez said to him. "The ones still living smoked out. The rest are dead."

Kade approached them, covered in demon ichor, tucking his pistol into its holster. He placed a comforting hand on Michael's shoulder. "I'm sorry. What he did was incredibly brave and selfless. He's a hero."

Michael looked to where the breach had been between

the worlds, to where his brother's lifeless body lay in the sand. "He's everyone's hero. They just don't know it."

It took hours to burn the bodies. If there was anything left the next day, the tour guides would surely assume some kids had snuck onto the island at night to have a party and the ash piles and debris were nothing more than the remains of their bonfire.

The two men Kade had lost in the fight had separate funeral pyres. They'd given their lives for the protection of their kind, and everyone felt burning them with the demons would be wrong. When they were done, the remaining party of seven boarded the boat and headed back to the mainland.

CHAPTER FORTY

Dez

The next day, Deziree and Vegas arrived back at her apartment. They were exhausted and overwhelmed by the last few days' events. Kade and his men had gone back to their respective homes after exchanges of thanks all around. Deziree flopped onto the bed, never having been so glad to lie there as she did after the trip. Vegas stood in her bedroom doorway, leaning against the wooden frame. He had been quiet the entire trip back, no doubt mourning his brother. She wished she knew the words to make him feel better, but she knew it was a lost cause. Vegas had spent so much of his time irritated with his brother for one immature, selfish act after another. Losing Lucas the way he did not only hurt but caused a lot of guilt. Guilt because he'd never had enough faith in his brother to believe he'd truly changed. She knew because she'd felt the same way.

"What now?" Vegas finally asked.

"Now," she replied, patting the spot next to her on the bed, signaling for him to join her, "we rest. It's been a long week." Vegas walked over and sat on the bed next to her.

"Has it really only been a week? It feels like it's been a year."

They sat in contented silence, but it was broken by her cell phone ringing. The caller ID read, *Cassandra*. She stared at the number on the screen and recognition dawned. Blurry numbers on an illuminated cell phone screen. Numbers she'd been trying to work out in her head ever since she'd seen a brief glimpse of them in one of Asmodeus's memories. The memory and the screen in front melded into one and the numbers were a perfect match.

"Son of a bitch!" she screamed. Rage, shock, and hurt filled her all at once.

"What is it?" Vegas asked urgently.

"We need to go back to Venice," Deziree growled. "Right now."

CHAPTER FORTY-ONE

Dez

As they walked up the front steps of the estate in Venice, Deziree's nerves were raw. Never in a million years did she think she would be here about to make an accusation of this magnitude. Vegas walked beside her, the predator in him showing is his every step. When she had told him why they needed to go to Venice, he was as startled as she was. Since then, anger had replaced surprise. She had answered the phone and told Cassandra to call the Council, letting her know they were on their way back to Venice. In a bluff of sorts, she told Cass to be careful who she trusted. They needed her to stay right where she was.

They stepped through the front door and one of the butlers let them know the Council was waiting. They thanked the man and showed themselves to the meeting room.

Without hesitation or attention paid to manners, they barged in through the double doors. The entire Council startled in unison and Cassandra jumped to her feet.

"Deziree," she said in a polite greeting. "Please, come in."

"Can it, Cass," Deziree replied, completely cold.

"Pardon me?" Cassandra asked.

One of the Council members spoke up. "What is the meaning of this?" Deziree disregarded the question.

"We've been busy," Deziree said. "I have to admit I haven't been completely honest with you. I told you we were going to try to see if we could dig up any leads. What I didn't tell you is that the demon being here did something to me."

"What do you mean? What's happened to you?" Cassandra eyed Deziree, not really sure where she was going with her explanation.

"Let's just say I've developed certain abilities. Seems having my *father* around triggered something in me." She braced her hands on the table, staring daggers at Cassandra.

"Your father?"

"Drop the act," Deziree replied. "You know damn well he was my father. After all, you're the one who summoned him. By name."

As soon as the words were out, quiet murmurs filled the air as the Council members focused on Cassandra.

"When I finally realized it," Dez continued, "it made sense. Thinking back to the last Council meeting, you knew something you shouldn't have known."

Cassandra stood and started to walk toward Deziree. "Me? Why would I—"

"Don't move!" Deziree snapped. "Not one step further!" Cassandra obeyed. "I saw it, Cass. We paid a visit to the home of the records keeper the last night we were in Venice. When I touched the spot where Natalia was murdered, I connected to the demon's memories. I saw him rape, torture, and finally murder that poor girl. You knew she was tortured. You mentioned it when you informed the Council of the demon's presence. The final clue was your phone number."

Deziree pulled her phone out of her pocket and held it in the air. "See, after we left Venice, we went on a trip. The memories of Natalia's murder told me where the Guardians were. We went to each murder scene and I repeated the process, pulling those memories as well. The demon made a phone call after he killed the Guardian in Savannah. I would have known right then, but I couldn't quite focus on the phone number in the memory. The numbers were too blurry. Well, the memory from the last Guardian told me where the demon was going to open the gateway. We went there and we put Asmodeus down, but not before he opened the portal and allowed a few hundred demons to pour out. Maybe more. We don't really know."

Murmurs filled the air again.

"Don't worry," Deziree said. "The gateway is closed again. Lucas Tremayne gave his own life to be sure of that. When I got a phone call from you, I saw your number flash across the screen on my phone and the memory from the Savannah house suddenly became clear as crystal. I saw your number and knew you had been the one Asmodeus had called. It was you."

"Cassandra?" Klaudia stood. "Is this true?"

Cassandra stood in silence for a long moment, then her posture changed, a concerned look on her face replaced by one of irritation.

"Lucas Tremayne," she scoffed. "I should have known he was fucking her. We knew someone had been at her apartment after she was dealt with but we didn't know who. I should have figured. No woman ever runs the chance of having cold sheets when he's in Venice." Vegas took a step forward and Dez shot out a hand to stop him.

"Probably just as well he's dead. That man was a waste of perfectly good fangs."

This time Vegas released a deep warning growl.

Deziree shook her head at Cassandra, tears welling in her eyes. "I don't understand it. What happened to you, Cass? Why would you do this?"

"Nothing happened to me," Cassandra replied. "I opened my eyes. The end of days is coming. Every religion the world around has a doomsday prophecy of some sort. They might not get the details right, but the basic tale is there. You make your allegiance and may the best side win! Do you think their god is going to take pity on vampires? Or witches? And what about you?" She pointed at Deziree and cocked her head. "How do you think a half-breed like yourself will fare in the final fight? I decided to make a preemptive strike. Long ago, I aligned with the side most likely to accept us. I set things in motion for the demons to break free from Hell and when the time comes, we would have someone fighting for us instead of all sides fighting against us. I did it for the good of the covens."

"You don't have the right to make that choice for every vampire and witch. Who they will side with is their decision. Demons owe no one fealty, no matter what favors you grant them. They have no honor, Cassandra. They would have burned you the first chance they got."

"You're wrong. The demons would have honored their agreement. They needed me. I alone have set into motion a series of events that cannot be stopped."

"If they need you so bad, then where are they now?" Cassandra didn't answer. "You've betrayed everyone in this room, and every witch and vampire in the world."

"I did what was necessary. When the time comes, you'll see that I was right. You'll see that I chose the winning side for the sake of our kind."

Dez walked to Vegas and put a hand on his cheek. She

leaned up and gave him a kiss. When she pulled away, she looked into his eyes, willing him to understand.

"There's no turning back now. I love you," she whispered, "and I am sorry."

He opened his mouth to respond and his words caught in his throat as her eyes turned completely black in a split second. She whirled on Cassandra. "For the blood on your hands, you must pay with your life." Deziree tipped her head and Cassandra immediately doubled over.

"It doesn't matter what you do to me," Cassandra said with maniacal laughter. "Fate cannot be bested."

Deziree reached for the hellfire with her mind and commanded her new power with a comfortable ease. Cassandra collapsed to the floor, screams replacing laughter as her body burst into flames. She howled as her body writhed and twisted, trying to escape from the anguish caused by the supernatural flames. As quickly as it started, it was over. Silence came and Cassandra was gone.

Suddenly, an orange beam of light broke down through the ceiling and poured into Deziree's body. When it disappeared, she could feel the demonic essence infusing itself into every fiber of her being. Every demonic ability previously unavailable to her was there at her fingertips, potent and effortless.

Vegas's eyes were fixed on her, frozen in shock. She could feel herself dissolving, changing until she disappeared into a cloud of black smoke and vanished into the ether. As she moved to the door, the room broke out into frantic panic. Vegas searched for her. He ran to the door and looked out but he couldn't see her. She took one last look at him, fighting every urge to shift back to solid form and touch him again.

Things had irrevocably changed. Moving forward meant leaving Venice but she had no idea where she would go. Maybe if she went back to New York and waited out the storm, she could find Vegas later and figure something out.

In the ether, she floated away from the estate and found a secluded alley a few blocks away. In the alley, she shifted back to her corporeal form and stepped out onto the street to hail a cab. As she climbed into the car that stopped for her, she glanced back in the direction of the estate. She didn't know where she stood with the covens. She didn't know where she stood with Vegas. She couldn't even be sure what she was anymore.

Vegas ... I'm so sorry, she wished she could say to him. She'd apologize a thousand times more if it meant they could be together.

She curled against the cab's back seat.

Until we meet again ...

NEXT IN THE SERIES

SOME SECRETS ARE BETTER OFF LOCKED AWAY.

Dez is on the run from the covens. Nearly six months have passed since her father, the demon Asmodeus, opened a gateway allowing countless of his kind to spill onto our plane of existence. Using her newfound abilities to hunt down the strays, Dez's life has become a never-ending cycle of violence and bloodshed, punctuated by the paranoia of constantly looking over her shoulder for the Council's vampire assassin.

When she receives an unexpected phone call from an old friend, Dez makes her way to the northern Arizona desert. There she finds a message waiting for her from beyond the grave, a message forcing her to confront the one thing she's been dreading for months.

Now Dez is haunted by a ghost from her past and faced with the secret truth of her origins. With her life and the lives of countless humans hanging in the balance, she's forced to face off with an enemy she doesn't even know exists. It's time to choose her destiny and the clock is running out.

BOOKS BY JENA GREGOIRE

~ Urban Fantasy & Paranormal Romance Author ~

THE HELLFIRE SERIES

THE DEVIL YOU KNOW

SPEAK OF THE DEVIL

DANCE WITH THE DEVIL

THE EXECUTIONER SERIES

BAD WOLF

A Hellfire Spin-Off Series

MORE IN THE HELLFIRE WORLD

VANISHING

A Hellfire Novella

BURNING

A Hellfire Prequel Short Story

SUFFERING

A Hellfire Short Story

RECKONING

An Executioner Prequel Novella

ABOUT THE AUTHOR

Internationally bestselling author **JENA GREGOIRE** was born and raised in New Hampshire, USA, and despite her abhorrence for any season which dares to drop to a temperature below seventy degrees, she still currently resides there with her two children and several furbabies. Always a passionate reader, her love of urban fantasy books inevitably morphed into a love of writing them. She is currently working on the *Hellfire* series and the *Executioner* series, a *Hellfire* world spin off series.

JenaGregoire.com

Made in the USA
Columbia, SC
06 August 2023